BONNIE ENGSTROM

Doreen Finds Her Groove

The Candy Cane Girls, book 8

By Bonnie Engstrom

Copyright © 2019 Bonnie Engstrom

Forget Me Not Romances, a division of Winged Publications.

All rights reserved as permitted under the U.S. Copyright Act of 1976. No part of the publication may be reproduced, distributed or transmitted in any form or by any means, or stored in a database or retrieval system, without prior permission of the publisher.

All verses from NIV version

This book is a work of fiction. Names, characters, places, and incidents are the product of the author's imagination and are used fictitiously. Any resemblance to actual events, locales, or persons, living or dead, is coincidental, except for the instances where they were used in conjunction with a business on purpose.
All rights reserved.

ISBN-13: 979-8-3302-5713-3

This book is dedicated to Lisa Arnott, the mom Happy Arthur rescued.

Thank you

This is always the hard part because there are so many people to thank.

My husband Dave good-naturedly held up countless dinners he cooked while I tapped on my keyboard.

Cynthia Hickey, publisher extra ordinaire, has been extremely patient, too. I can't thank either of them enough.

Friend and award-winning author Alice K. Arenz for encouragement and prayers.

Jesus. I petitioned Him so many times for suggestions how to make this story work. Without His comfort and guidance I would still be tapping on the keyboard. Thank you, Lord.

WHAT OTHERS SAY ABOUT BONNIE ENGSTROM'S BOOKS

(about *Noelle's Christmas Wedding*)

"I was moved from the very first line. There is a lot of attention to detail in this book. Imaginative, real and believable." Amazon Review

"Bonnie Engstrom never disappoints her readers. Her stories are lively, intriguing and keep me guessing. The characters are like actual people, warm and appealing, someone I would like in real life. She catches my attention on the first page and holds it to the end. I'm always anxious for the next book."
~ Barbara Warren, author of *Hidden Danger*, an inspirational romantic suspense.

(about *Restoring Love at Christmastime*, a 5 Star Readers Favorite)

"I'm not normally a reader of romance novels. . . Even though some readers might find the premise of renewing a teen romance from years earlier, one that never really had much of a chance to get started, a bit unbelievable, the author skillfully convinced me to believe and accept that.

I especially appreciated the Christian elements in the story. And the humor. And the animals. And the humor related to the animals. (I say that to avoid giving a spoiler.)

I was torn between four stars and five. Although I didn't love it as much as some novels I've read, I liked it too much just to say I liked it. So I'm rating it the way I think I would do if I were a hardened romance buff."

~ Roger Bruner, author of *Rosa No-Name*.

(about *Butterfly Dreams*)

"I enjoyed this book as well as a couple of other books of Bonnie's that I've had the chance to read! Someday I'd really enjoy the chance to meet her in person!" 5 Star Amazon Review

"A wonderful page turner as you walk through the chapters discovering her most intimate thoughts, fears and happiness." 5 Star Amazon Review

"Bonnie Engstrom gives us a humorous, sometimes irreverent, often heart touching look at romance through the eyes of fifty something Betsy. . . the author succeeds in proving that 'Love is a gift at any age.'"

~ Sharon Srock, author of *Women of Valley View* and *Sisters of Design* series.

"A lovely weaving of romance, forgiveness and encouragement are the words that best describe this lovely novel from author Bonnie Engstrom."

~ Award winning author Kathi Macias, author of *Special Delivery* and *The Deliverer.*

ABOUT THE CANDY CANES

Years ago, six high school freshmen in Newport Beach, California formed a swim team that became legendary. They won the state relay swim championship four years in a row. In addition to their skill and devotion to daily practicing, they prayed together and vowed to be sisters forever. Another thing that set them apart was they chose their own swimsuits making them a team within a larger team. They chose red and white diagonally striped swimsuits. Thus, became known as the Candy Canes. They always will be.

Dear Reader ~

I hope you will enjoy this series that tells the stories of women who are what I call super friends ~ friends who committed as teenagers to prayer and loyalty bound by a moniker. The Candy Cane Girls are a unique group of sister friends. I hope their stories will inspire other young women. They are Sisters of Promise, promises they made when young and promises they've kept for generations.

I am hoping to start an inspiration, a situation or a way to encourage young women, especially teen girls, to write their own stories. I have three teenage granddaughters who are bright and talented but as far as I know do not record their thoughts and experiences. I also pray for other teen girls of friends. It troubles me they are not writing about their lives and experiences. Please join me in praying for an upcoming of young women writers.

As you read through this series, and I hope you will, please note how each book tells a story about individual women, how each struggle with a personal situation and overcomes it. Some of the circumstances they encounter are destined by faith and fate; but all require belief and commitment to each other and to the faith of each. I hope you will read every story to see how Cindy deals with her new love's health issues, and Candy takes her fears into action, and Connie . . . well she has a problem that she overcomes with the help of sweet Jake, her 'problems solving' dog. Jake will appear in many following books. He was my running companion for many years – the dearest dog. But Lola and Happy Arthur are shining woofers in their own stories.

But wait until you get to Natalie and Melanie! They hold the keys to lasting friendship. Their stories are almost legendary.

All stories in the series can be read individually, but you will enjoy them more and understand them more if you read them in order.

Noelle, Cindy, Connie, Candy, Natalie, Doreen and especially Melanie will steal your heart.
You will have fun with the different wedding venues. How many weddings have you attended in an historical place, or in a hospital lobby or a gym? Maybe these will be your first and most memorable.

You will do me a great favor if you enjoyed this series and write a quick, honest review on Amazon or Goodreads. Just a few words mean a lot and encourage others to read it.

Thank you. If you would like to be connected to me for comments and conversation please sign up for my newsletter at www.bonnieengstrom.com and learn about my writing history. You can email me at bengstrom@hotmail.com. Please put SERIES <in caps) in the subject line. I would love to chat with you.

Special BONUS! The Candy Cane Series is ideal

for group discussion, especially for book clubs. I have a special offer for book clubs for all of my books. If you are interested please email me at bengstrom@hotmail.com with CLUB <all caps) in the subject line.

Blessings,
Bonnie

BONNIE ENGSTROM

Prologue

Doreen jiggled the latch on her boot, the one on her shorter left leg. Why wouldn't it snap? Her calf ached from the effort. She had done this a hundred times, well maybe a few dozen. Why did she always second guess herself and attempt to be so literal? She shook her head and hooked a fingernail under the errant latch, and it finally lifted and snapped.

Whew, five tries. Not too bad. Why is the phone ringing at six a.m.? Grabbing her cellphone from the bathroom vanity she punched the accept button.

BONNIE ENGSTROM

ONE

She couldn't do this. Not now, not when Winning Designs Boutique was having a huge promotion with all its couture samples on sale. She was depended upon as the manager. Plus she had a modeling gig in two days. An important one highlighting women with disabilities. In L.A. What would Connie and Jaeda think if she ran off suddenly to get married?

"No, Bill, not the right time." She wiped a tear with a manicured finger and almost stabbed her right eye. Grabbing a tissue, she blotted the eye and blinked. Today must be her clumsy day.

She had waited so long for this, knew he had, too. But it was not the right time.

"So . . ." His voice sounded irritated. "When exactly is that?"

"I . . . I don't know. Not sure, but not now."

She stared at the phone disbelieving his words. Bill never cursed, but he just did.

~

Bill Lord, Jr. swore again, but this time he

swore at himself.

"What am I doing, Lord? Why can't I wait just a little longer?" He whispered, he hoped to God, but lately he wasn't sure.

He picked up the phone and blurted, "Sorry. Insensitive of me."

"Sorry, too." Her voice was tearful.

He had a sudden vision of the woman he loved, an almost ethereal vision. She was floating in space. A long soft gown of lavender billowed around her. Glittering silver shoes graced her lovely feet. He looked closely and could see the corrective insert in the left one. He knew about it, but was sure no one else did. Doreen glided down the walkway beaming to guests on both sides who smiled and silently clapped. Not appropriate to clap during a modeling event. He knew that. But since he wasn't present in this vision, this dream, he clapped. Loudly. Doreen turned to him and smiled, her wonderful warm and loving smile. He shook his head and awoke to words coming from his cellphone.

"How about next Saturday?" the wobbly voice said.

"You sure? Is that all right with Connie?" He respected, even loved Connie and Jaeda the owners of Winning Designs Boutique in Corona del Mar, but he was getting impatient. Mostly with Doreen. Was she having cold feet? Fear of marriage? Fear of their love for each other?

"Yes." Doreen's voice was stronger now.

It gave him hope. He had waited too many years to hold her in his arms and claim his love for her. Was she reluctant because of her disability or plain old fear?

"Yes," Doreen repeated. "She is excited for us. She and Jaeda will come here with the twins and monitor the shop. Plus, she will design my gown, and she will be my matron of honor. The woman is amazing!"

"That is pretty amazing to do all that in a week and a half." Bill rubbed his forehead. "You sure she can do that?"

"Her seamstress lives nearby, the twins are sleeping longer in the night, Jaeda has the long weekend off." Doreen took a breath. "I believe she can. Connie is a whirlwind of energy, thrives on deadlines. She even keeps a huge stash of fabrics in her workroom. All will be well, Billy."

He cringed at the nickname, knew it was a loving one. But ever since he was twelve, he hated it. Billy, Billy Junior, Little Bill. Dad was always Big Bill. What was he?

He strived hard to be himself, to overcome the bullying. He'd won the international modeling contest barely out of his teens with a case of chicken pox, the scabs covering him liberally, even with Richard's thick makeup. Richard Stevens, co-owner of Stevens and Crosse Cosmetics almost around the corner in Newport, had become his temporary savior. Entering the contest was a huge risk, but his agent, Madeline, insisted. He squirmed on the long plane ride to Germany hoping he wouldn't give the disease to other passengers. Ugh. Talk about guilt.

Bill rubbed his leg where one spot still itched, even after twelve years. He still questioned how he won the contest in New York City, then Germany, then was sent to Italy to be the promo model for Ducati. He had always loved cycles, and Ducati was the primo of the world. But when the company capitalized on his last name to insinuate Bill Lord was sitting astride a heavenly cycle in the huge billboards, that God had conferred holy favor on the man and cycle because of his name, that's when he quit. It was not a label he wanted to be a party to. He'd considered suing the company for defamation, but his dad said to let it go. Bill had made a lot of money from those ads, money he donated and invested for a future. Dad was right, as always.

Then he bumped into friends of the girl of his dreams in the supermarket of all places. He'd been looking for pasta when his cart banged into theirs. "Haven't we met before?"

Their smiles did it. Looking back, he realized the three girls were all Candy Cane friends, but none had been Doreen. How had he met Doreen? Was his mind so muddled?

He rubbed the itch on his leg again and went to take a shower. The cold water stung his skin.

Ten days. In less than two weeks he would hold his love in his arms forever.

TWO

Doreen kicked off the stuffy boots and rubbed her stockinged feet. Why did she insist on wearing them? The one with the orthopedic lift in it kept her off balance. The new lift was thicker than her others. She should probably go back to the podiatrist and have it re-made. She'd heard adjustable ones were now available. The appointment took time, and remaking the insert would, too. Time. Something she had little of recently.

But she hated to stumble, knew it made her look . . . well, sometimes drunk. That was the worst. So embarrassing. It had happened several weeks ago during mid-afternoon. She had just finished a yummy Sashimi lunch of her favorite salmon with pickled salad on the side at Kitayama's sushi bar. It had been her day to treat herself after a long, challenging morning with a diva at the boutique who ordered gowns for all her bridesmaids. She was on her way back for the appointment with the

Mother of the Bride, the MOB as most in the wedding business dubbed her, when a Newport Beach Police car pulled next to her Lexus in the restaurant parking lot.

He flashed his badge. He explained another patron, anonymous of course, called the police about an inebriated woman about to drive. She showed him her license, the one with her disability stated on it, even started to remove her boot to show him the insert. The young officer blushed, apologized and left. But the police car trailed her back to her parking space behind the boutique. It was obvious since the small parking area in the back was in a dirt alley. Not a normal roadway for a cop car to venture to, unless there was a problem.

Doreen pulled off the sock from her boot foot and stuck her hand in it and used it to wipe her damp forehead. Why was she stressing about a situation that had happened almost months ago? Or, was she still worrying about Billy's love for her?

They had met when Natalie called her and Melanie to come see and meet the two Bills in Nat's Gym. Two gorgeous guys, father and son, both handsome. She couldn't remember why they had shown up in the small neighborhood gym, but she did remember that day. Bill, Sr. was a tall, bulky, handsome man with thinning gray hair and an imposing personality. His son, who was briefly introduced as Bill, Jr., was to die for gorgeous. She found out later he was an international model for a renowned Italian motorcycle company. She almost passed out when he called her after he approached her in the gym. She had been scared, but her Candy

Cane friends and their prayers gave her courage. Doreen and Bill's first date was more than just a beginning. On a motorcycle.

Hopefully, it would be a glorious one for another beginning.

BONNIE ENGSTROM

Three

Was she doing the right thing? Was she sure? Doreen grabbed the hair at the back of her head and scrunched it hard. Sometimes that brought focus, but not this morning. It just hurt.

She wasn't due to open the shop for another two hours. Not hungry, she nixed the breakfast idea. Maybe she could fill the time dreaming about and planning her own wedding. She chuckled about the random thought. She had been planning it since she was nine, more than two decades ago. Then twelve years ago the almost fatal accident happened just a block from Hoag Hospital in Newport Beach. Five plus hours of surgery on her leg, leaving it shorter. Forgiving Melanie. Connie offering her a modeling career. But as a gimp? She knew that was a derogatory term, but that's what she'd felt like. With no other options she accepted. Now she was renowned internationally. Not just as a model for women with disabilities, but as a woman. Tall, lithe, slender, and beautiful is what the promos in the papers and ads said. Right now she felt short, clumsy, and overweight.

She took a sucking breath and pushed open her closet door. At least she could look for shoes to wear to her own wedding. Maybe the silver ones she'd worn for Connie's wedding, and Melanie's and Noelle's and Cindy's and Candy's. And sweet Emily's, the crazy avant-garde designer who married Nick the surfer in Nat's Gym.

Would they still fit? Would the orthopedic insert still work? They were almost a tradition now, those shoes worn for so many friends' weddings. They could be her something old. Perfect to wear for her own wedding.

The sling backs still worked catching her heel in the right place, even on the shorter leg. She wobbled around the bedroom testing them. Maybe if she lost five pounds before her wedding they would be okay. They were classically beautiful and held so much meaning, especially for Connie. She chuckled how Connie shared with the other girls about rubbing Jaeda's leg under a table at Starbucks to get his attention. Boy was that man smitten. Even his little dog Jake drooled over Connie. What a fun memory. Doreen hoped the other Candy Canes would have lovely memories of her romance and her wedding.

Something new was obvious. Her gown. Connie's designs were always spectacular and unique. She'd asked Doreen for her preferences. After all, it was the bride's choice, as Doreen well knew from all the titillating, nervous brides she had assisted at Winning Designs. Many were made far more nervous by their mothers who always had strong opinions, usually diverse from their bride daughters.

She thought about Connie's questions. "Long, short, flowing, swinging?" and "Your favorite color? Pastel, deep, fading from light to dark?" Maybe she had answered them too abruptly, and she hoped Connie wasn't offended.

"I'm sorry, Con. Have no definite desires. Not sure this is such a good idea, after all."

"What? Getting married? Or, getting married to Bill?"

Doreen sucked in her breath and wiped tears dripping on her closet carpet. "Both of the above, I guess. The timing seems so off, but Bill is pushing."

She wasn't surprised when she heard Connie sigh. Connie was a big sigher. Maybe that's how she let stress out, maybe that's what Doreen should learn to do. Breathe in through the nose and whoosh out through the mouth. She tried it. Seemed to relieve tension, at least a little.

"What are you doing, Doreen?" Connie must have heard her. Was she that loud? A spate of giggles and whooshing back and forth left Doreen collapsed on the floor of her closet holding her tummy.

"So needed that, Con. Thank you."

"My pleasure."

That set them off again until one of the twins cried loudly.

"Oops. Mel must need her diaper changed. She hates to be wet. Gotta go," Connie said as she hung up.

Doreen fingered the strap of the silver shoes. Was she doing the right thing? She loved Bill, and she believed he loved her. She had even to her dismay asked Melanie to take a ride with him a few months ago on his motorcycle, to pretend Melanie was scared and to question Bill about his love for her.

But, now? Was now the right time? She put the shoes back in the box labeled Silver-Wedding and shoved the box on the shelf. Her foot still hurt, actually her leg, from the boots. Maybe it was time to re-evaluate her decision. Too hasty? But Bill was excited, and planning. She pressed on.

Something borrowed? That could be anything from one of the other girls, even her groom she laughed. She needed that joke on herself. Melanie had gone gaga over both Bills. Doreen had had no interest in either. Until the encounter at Nat's Gym while she was lifting free weights in front of the mirrors. She'd been barely aware someone was watching her, and it made her uncomfortable when Bill, Jr. approached her and introduced himself. He'd handed her a business card and asked for her phone number. She was glad she'd asked Nat about him later. Didn't hurt she was captivated by his gorgeous azure eyes. So much for history.

She opened the jewelry drawer in the corner cabinet, the one that held her mother's few necklaces and bracelets, mostly costume, except one. Twisting the small diamond on her finger she held her breath. Her mom never had a diamond engagement ring. She'd actually bought herself a diamond in her fifties when she worked part-time in a jewelry store. That simple ring with the less than a carat stone is what she would borrow. She would wear it on the little finger of her right hand. A tribute to her mom. She put it back in the drawer. Closing the drawer she reminisced how as a child she'd dressed up in Mom's brown suit, the one she'd secretly gotten married in. It was the closest to wedding attire she had. Doreen had climbed the stairs to the attic, rooted through boxes and trunks to finally retrieve it, to feel its warmth, to pretend. The cabinet drawer clicked shut.

Blue had to be a garter. Cindy's was almost legendary having been caught by Rob after Noelle and Braydon's wedding. Should she borrow Cindy's or buy a new one. She would ask.

Well, that's all planned. But, why did she still feel so unsettled? Probably nerves. She went downstairs to have some strawberry yogurt. That counted as breakfast, didn't it?

BONNIE ENGSTROM

Four

Bill needed to talk to his dad. Lately Big Bill was so involved with Vivian and all the fun excursions they were doing, he wondered if Dad was available. He called.

"Son! So glad to hear from you. What's up?" Bill, Sr. always jumped right to the chase, to the core.

His dad's reaction seemed a bit odd since they talked several times a week. But he let it go. "I need advice, Dad."

"Of course. I can help." Why did Dad always assume? Always think his advice was best? Wasn't that why Bill called?

"Gonna get married." There, he'd said it. Simple.

"Whew, finally." He heard Dad take a breath. "I hope it's that lovely Doreen."

Bill almost choked. Dad was so perceptive. Or maybe it was obvious.

"Uh, what should I wear? Also, any ideas about

where to honeymoon? Or, anything?"

After the loud guffaw, he heard a sweet feminine voice. Vivian? Dad always passed complicated questions off to her. Were his questions that complicated?

"Hello, dear. I just heard the fabulous news. About time!" she giggled. "What can I help you with?"

Bill was grateful for his step-mom, and knew she was up on protocol. He plunged ahead with his list of questions. Couldn't hurt.

Twenty minutes later, after listing Vivian's answers and ideas on his iPad, he looked them over. Almost all of them said, "Ask the bride."

Five

Doreen threw the book against the wall. Followed by a boot.

What was she thinking reading a book about how to do a wedding? She'd helped hundreds of brides select and design gowns. She'd listened to all the back and forth banter and suggestions. She'd been a bridesmaid in so many Candy Cane weddings she had almost lost count. The other morning in her closet she'd figured out the old, new, borrowed, and blue. But she hadn't decided where to hold the wedding. And Bill had never asked.

Noelle's had been in the famous Sherman Foundation Gardens, Connie's in the historic Balboa Pavilion, Candy's in a preschool church, but Cindy's was the most spectacular on the beach in Costa Rica where she and Rob were sent by Mariners church to plant a church on a remote Central American beach. Emily's had been in Nat's Gym. Not so simple as many thought it would be, but a spectacular extravagance. Poor Melanie's was held in the lobby of a hospital – gorgeous, but with a sad result.

Maybe she should decide for Rogers Gardens where Vivian and Bill married. It was filled with lush foliage, lots of color, and had a renowned restaurant. That could be the perfect venue. But it wasn't her own, Bill's and her own.

~

Bill wanted to have a part in it. Weren't they a team? He understood Vivian's comments about tradition, but this is the twenty-first century. Shouldn't he have some input, a say?

He thought about all the places they'd loved together, the fun they'd had on rides at the Fun Zone on Balboa, the joy they'd shared walking on Big Corona Beach. Neither of those said wedding. He knew Doreen should have a very special wedding in a very special place. She deserved it. She had been through so much with the tragedy of her accident twelve years ago. Still she had gained so much as a model for Connie's designs, being the manager and exclusive model for Winning Designs, being the one in charge of day-to-day operations. Most important, thinking back to Vivian's comments, Doreen is the bride. Surely, he could deal with that. Was his own ego intact?

Six

She went to her thinking place. Ordered a Venti pineapple infusion tea. Holding her phone steady, she sipped and scrolled. Scrolled more. Nothing came up to entice her on the *Stu News* online newspaper. It had so many ads and ideas, but no inspiration. It had to be someplace very special, a place they would remember forever, a place to hold in their hearts. Sighing, she dropped her phone on the table and sipped.

Suddenly it came to her. What? The market where she shopped and bought the beautiful flowers, the ones on sale every weekend? No, not a possibility. No supermarket would do that, would it? She received the market's little magazine every month with lots of coupons in it. Must be because she was a frequent shopper. It probably tracked her loyalty card. So much for privacy.

She thought about Steve who was the master of flower knowledge in the market's floral department. She loved to stop and chat with him and ask his advice about orchids. Before Connie and Jaeda offered her the manager position at Winning Designs she had applied online to work with Steve. No positions in that market were available, only others in the huge chain, too far away to consider. But she knew Steve's ability to produce gorgeous floral arrangements, even for weddings. She had seen them. Still, she always had Braydon from Love In Bloom who had gifted all the other Candy Canes with his bridal bouquets. No, it would not be right to ignore tradition. Braydon would be offended, so would Noelle. Besides, the supermarket wasn't a special place for her and Bill together. But a fun idea. She kept scrolling.

~

Bill wanted to help, wanted to be part of the decision. Vivian had told him that wasn't his role, unless Doreen asked. It hardly mattered since he hadn't thought of any clever ideas or perfect place to have their wedding. Still he deliberated. How much would it matter if they copied? What if they had their wedding in the same place as one of the other Candy Cane couples? Each place had been spectacular, but each place had memories of one couples' romance and wedding, theirs alone. Even Nick and Emily's in Nat's Gym of all places. It had been super fun, but very unusual and unconventional. No way did he want to repeat Melanie and Larry's place in the lobby of a hospital. Especially since Larry was arrested almost an hour after. Not good vibes!

As far as he knew his and Doreen's wedding would be the last Candy Cane one, unless Natalie actually found love. Poor Natalie. Love always seemed to escape her. That, if it ever happened, would be special.

Bill forced himself back to the moment, his own wedding with Doreen. He wasn't a fan of so-called venue weddings where the guests had to travel, sometimes with great expense, to attend. Everyone had done it for Cindy and Rob's wedding on the beach in Costa Rica. That was different. It had been worth the expense to experience that beautiful country, to see chattering monkeys hanging from trees who dropped onto their shoulders to grin, to ride high above the lush forest in a zip line. And, of course, to be part of their vows looking out at the gorgeous Pacific with all the children in attendance. Dana's four kids and Brian's two boys, plus Lucy the dog. He would never forget the mild ocean breeze blowing his hair and little Shyla literally tossing flower petals. But, when Rob almost lost it emotionally declaring his love for Cindy, he almost lost it, too.

Bill wanted different, special for Doreen. He kept scrolling.

He wanted something unique for Doreen. Many of the Candy Cane women had married in Newport Beach; some in historic or famous places like gardens lush with flowers. Those always lent to the atmosphere of a wedding celebration. Custom made. But Bill wanted lavish. Over the top for Doreen. Extravagant. He could afford it, knew Dad would support him both in fantasy and financially. That wasn't necessary, though, since Bill was independently secure, thanks to the Italian motorcycle company. He Googled hotels and was astounded. Never having to stay in a hotel in the area, he hadn't realized how many were there. He checked out all the websites, learned many had been taken over by huge corporate chains. He decided to visit each one, feel the ambiance, talk with the event coordinators, get a personal feel for each place. At least that wouldn't be intrusive.

The first was a sweet little venue on Lido Aisle. Sadly, as much as he liked it, too small. The second enticed him. The Fashion Island Hotel was astounding. Fabulous, gorgeous, the perfect place to celebrate. Expensive, yes, but so worth it for Doreen. Would she agree? As famous as she was in her modeling career, she was humble, and low-keyed. She avoided fanfare and notoriety. She told him once she didn't keep all the newspaper clippings and social media posts about her. She said it wasn't about her, but about God who gave her this. Surely, she would see he, Bill, wanted to gift this to her. Wouldn't she?

Seven

Doreen clicked on the email again. Surely Bill was spoofing, teasing her. The Fashion Island Hotel was more than opulent, over the top, extravagant. She would be expected to look and act extravagant. She hated being in the spotlight. Stupid, considering she modeled on runways in other countries and never blinked an eye and never sweat. She called Natalie. Nat would have advice.

Nat was typical Nat, telling it like it is. No fluffs, no pretense, all down to earth.

"I'm sorry, Doreen. I guess I don't understand."

Doreen could almost see Natalie rubbing her brow. Maybe Nat didn't understand. Her life was so different from Doreen's as the owner and guru of Nat's Gym where she gave Zumba classes and encouraged others to fine tune their muscles and "press on." Their lives were so different, but their friendship was real and strong.

When Doreen was conflicted and confused

about accepting Connie's offer to model for her Winning Designs line, it was Natalie who had encouraged Doreen. Natalie who said, "What's to lose? Take the opportunity. If you don't flap your wings and fly, you will never know if you soared."

"But I stumble, trip. The insert in my shoe is uncomfortable, annoying. Sometimes on a 'walk' the models are required to spin and dance down the aisle.

"Yes, I've studied it. I know what's expected of me. I can't dance."

Doreen was sure she heard Natalie gasp, maybe even hold her nose. So dramatic, so not like Nat. But she did.

"Okay, let's sort this out, Dor. We both know Connie and Jaeda chose you to oversee Winning Designs, and it wasn't a small decision. They are both professional and make detailed financial decisions, especially with Jaeda's banking background. They seldom make mistakes." Doreen heard a sigh and chuckle before Natalie continued. "Well, we won't mention the twin debacle." She laughed again.

Doreen laughed, too, remembering how Connie, the *honest one* the Candy Canes had dubbed her, was afraid to tell Jaeda they were having twins. Thanks to their little dog Jake, who she tripped over several times, the truth came out. Emily, the wife of Shane Sullivan owner of Spine Scottsdale, picked up on it while Jaeda was waiting for Connie to finish her doctor-ordered physical therapy. They laughed again imagining the expression on Jaeda's face. Men, they decided, are often so clueless.

"Okay, girl, back to the facts," Natalie said. "I know you forgave Melanie for your injury, I believe you accepted God's blessing. Now," she sighed, "what's the problem?"

"I told you. I . . . I'm clumsy."

"Not when you are prancing down the aisle of a major gig flinging the gossamer skirt you are wearing. And with glittering nails from your wonderful manicurist Kay. So what's up?"

"I can't dance."

Eight

Jaeda looked at the email Connie was sharing with him. "She wants to cancel the wedding plans? I don't understand."

"She's scared, Jaed. Not sure why, but I know she is." Connie jumped up to cuddle a twin, little Mel, who was having trouble sleeping. Her twin brother Larry was snoring, even at four months. "This is a big deal for Doreen, Jaed. I know you weren't there during her accident and all the trauma of almost six hours of surgery to save her leg."

"I've heard it was horrible from Noelle and Braydon, and of course Melanie who caused it. But I understand." He nodded. "We must be flexible for Doreen."

~

Doreen almost logged off her computer. She had been too embarrassed to call Connie. Email was less personal. Yet she was still uncomfortable. Connie hadn't let her down, she had let Connie down. Her wonderful friend, her employer, her personal angel.

Connie had saved her life in a way, especially her sanity. She had given her the gift of a future. Now she had a career. Hope. That's what Connie gave her. Confidence. Self-esteem. Doreen made a mental list and her eyes filled with tears. Now she was disappointing one of her dearest friends. She wiped the tears away with sparkling manicured fingers and looked at her hands. She'd never had a manicure before her accident. Her mom had suggested it for her before the senior prom. "Why?" she'd asked. No boy had invited her. She'd had no courage to ask a boy either. Not that she'd been attracted to any. Except Braydon Lovejoy from afar. The class cutup, the boy who had mooned Coach Wilson. The boy who was known for pulling pranks. The young man who she learned had led her friends in prayer while she was lying on a surgical table for almost six hours. Sometimes she was tempted to tell Noelle, sure that she would get a kick out of Doreen's youthful adoration. Or maybe not. She stared at her hands again.

She sent another email. "I am not a wimp, Con. It's all too sudden. No time to plan. So sorry."

She went back to her closet. All the things she'd planned for her wedding to Bill were still there in boxes and drawers. But her heart wasn't there. She needed her heart.

She recalled Melanie spouting off about Newport Beach and how over the top it was, almost fictional. How so many people with means, means she couldn't even imagine, showcased events, like weddings. Especially weddings. She'd never paid much attention, even as a teen, because swimming with the Candy Canes had been her life. Now her life would change dramatically when she took a vow to be Mrs. William Lord, Jr.

BONNIE ENGSTROM

Nine

Bill pushed the button on his phone again. Maybe he was reading the wrong text message. Nope. Backing out, again. She had seemed so sure, so excited. He almost decided to pretend he hadn't gotten the text. Cowardly! Not his style. He texted back.
    We need to talk in person. Fav place?

~

His vision of loveliness swept through the door. He waved from a tiny round table in the back corner. He remembered when he first saw her at Nat's Gym. She was lifting free weights and paid him no attention. His dad was on a treadmill being introduced to Candy and Melanie. Dad pulled him over to be introduced, too. Nice girls, both very pretty with long flowing hair. He hadn't paid much attention, just gave a courteous nod, then turned to glance at the tall, slender woman in the lavender tights. What was wrong with her leg? It had a stabilizing wrap on it. Yet, she was standing straight. When he turned back the other girls were gone. He would find out later they had swooned at his handsome dad. He was a little jealous. After all, he was the model. He rubbed his forehead now, ashamed at the egotistical memory. One that left him cold.

Doreen pulled open the glass door and approached slowly, then stopped to chat with a crowd of teen girls in school uniforms. She bent over a curly-haired one in a wheelchair and handed her something. The girl had looked so sad, but put on a fake smile for Doreen. Why was she taking so long? Then he saw her almost kneel, in Starbucks!

"What were you doing? Giving her a business card?"

"Mmm. Yes, and praying with her. Giving her a Bible verse to cling to."

"What verse? She is obviously crippled."

"Jeremiah 29:11. The one to give her hope."

Bill pulled her down and clasped her delicate hands. "What about hope for us?"

She withdrew her hands from his and stuffed them in her flowing skirt. "Sorry, Billy, can't do it. Not now."

"Why? You scared? Of what?" He wore his frustration and anger like a badge, and Doreen recoiled.

"Too soon. Can't explain. Can't dance."

"What? What does dancing have to do with us getting married. Make sense, Doreen."

~

She turned the shower on hot. Then cold, then hotter more. Didn't help. Her body still felt limp.

She had no pain in her shorter leg, only in her heart. Wasn't dancing an important part of a wedding reception? What would it look like if she didn't dance with her groom? Or her father? After turning off the light, she fluffed her pillow and wept.

Ten

Mom? Why was Mom calling her? They only spoke on Fridays after Doreen had closed the shop. Something was wrong.

"What's wrong, Mom? This is Tuesday and you're scaring me. Are you and Dad all right?"

The long pause scared her more. Mom never paused.

"Mom, what? What's wrong? Please."

Another pause, and a sigh. "Don't know quite how to say this, but . . ."

"But what?" Doreen had never known her mother to lack for words. Something was terribly wrong. She grabbed a tissue and held it to her face getting ready for the worst.

"I feel left out. No," she said in a wobbly voice, "I am left out."

"Of?"

"Okay, I will spill it." She heard her dad in the background hoarsely whispering "Tell her."

"I wanted to plan your wedding ever since you

were nine and dressed up in my brown suit. There, I've said it."

"Oh, Mom. I left you out."

"Yep. And my heart is broken."

Sad as it was Doreen had another excuse to cancel the imminent wedding. How could she have even forgotten about Mom's dreams? What a selfish daughter she was, an only daughter. She had gotten caught up in her own career, thoughtless of others, Mom and Bill. What had she become?

~

Bill slammed down the phone. Her mother? What does she have to do with planning their wedding? He called Dad, as he always did in emergencies. Was this one?

Dad passed the baton to Vivian.

"I'm sorry, Bill, but I'm surprised you question it. Also sorry Doreen didn't do the right thing by her mother. Maybe you young people are too independent?"

Vivian's words were spoken like a question. Were they too independent? Too into themselves? She hadn't said that, but the tone and inference was there. After all she'd gone through two marriages with Candy, so maybe she did have wisdom. And experience.

Self-reliant. That's what Vivian had implied. Not thinking about others.

Bill cupped his forehead in his hands. Was he really that selfish?

~

She needed help. Advice help and prayer help. She couldn't remember any of the Candy Canes' mothers planning their weddings. Did they? She called Kerstin Day, Noelle's mother, first.

"Yes, dear, I was behind the scenes, but I did all of the planning, made all of the arrangements with Jill the wonderful wedding coordinator. It was a gift to me, and to Noelle. It's what mothers do, what they dream of."

She hung up the phone sobbing. She had cheated her mother.

ELEVEN

Bill held her hand. He didn't know what to say so he squeezed tight. The Starbucks paper napkin would have to do. She grabbed it and blew into it hard.

"Sorry. Unladylike."

He hoped his hug would reassure her.

"What are you going to do?"

"I apologized of course. I sent Mom a plane ticket to come this weekend and took the time off. Natalie will fill in. I insisted she come. We need to spend time together. I've been so caught up in my job and modeling. So into myself.

"You do understand what this means?"

He did what Connie called the guy shrug. But he avoided Doreen's face and looked off into the distance. This Starbucks ceiling was no different than it used to be, but somehow he found solace in it. He rose abruptly, hugged Doreen tightly and waved.

"Gotta go. Research to do. Love you."

Doreen fiddled with the crumpled napkin and wiped her eyes again. Research? What research did Billy have to do? She needed help, so she called Vivian her future mother-in-law.

"Oh, dear." Vivian gasped the words. "Who needs help more? Bill, your mom, or you?"

Doreen wasn't sure how to answer the obviously rhetorical question. "I guess all of us. Can you give advice?"

She could almost see Vivian smiling. Who to choose? The woman was such a font of wisdom. The reply that came almost undid her.

"Well, sweetie, it's all on your shoulders. You offended, probably really hurt your mom. Now, you have sent Bill into back-off mode. He's scared. Needs to figure this out and start from the beginning.

"Lot of work and making up to do," she sighed loudly.

~

My fault, all my selfish fault.

Priorities. Moms were always on the top of the list. Isn't that what Vivian had hinted? She had stood by Candy twice, two weddings to the same man. But she never wavered. Strong woman, deep faith. Time for Doreen to be strong.

"You sure you want me?" Marion Zimmer posed the question.

Doreen did the "So sorry, of course I want you, *need* you." Was it enough? She had trouble getting her mind around it. She had always been close to mom, but in the last few years when she had so much responsibility one of them had drifted. Mom, or her?

She met mom at John Wayne Airport, hugged effusively, and picked up her bag.

"Why just a carryon?"

"Just for the weekend. Not staying long."

The phone call from Vivian came unexpected. Doreen had thought their conversation had concluded. Vivian hadn't called her before. She had always called Vivian.

Hoping nothing was wrong with Bill, Sr. or Vivian she picked up the phone.

"Hello, dear. Am I interrupting your evening?"

Vivian wanted to share the wedding plans with Mom! Would that work?

~

"I would love her help. She lives here and knows all the best. I remember meeting her briefly a few years ago. Isn't she one of the special girls' moms?"

"Yes, Candy's mom. She planned two of Candy's weddings to Will. Remember the story?" Marion nodded. "She also planned her own wedding to Bill Lord, Sr., my Bill's dad."

"Oh, my goodness!" Marion closed her eyes and blew out a breathless sigh. "That," she hesitated, "that means she will be your mother-in-law." It was Doreen's turn to nod, but with a wide grin. "You okay with that?"

"I love the idea, Mom, and I love Vivian. But the question is are you okay with it?"

Marion shifted in her chair. "I remember her as being a warm woman, but she will be here near you to go to for advice. I will be miles away."

What did that mean? Doreen shifted, too, and wrapped her arms around her mother and nestled her nose in Marion's neck. Hugging hard, she said, "Mom, no one will ever take your place. Ever." She hoped Mom believed her, but she noticed a tear on her mother's pale cheek.

The two composed themselves with lots of tissue wiping and hugging. Finally, Doreen pulled her mom up from the sofa. "Let's go to dinner, Mom. Do you still like sushi?"

Twelve

Marion fiddled with her salmon Sashimi, her favorite. She pushed it around on her plate with the chopsticks. Finally dipping it into the soy sauce and Wasabi combo she put it to her lips, then spit it out. "Sorry, but this is not salmon sashimi. What is it?"

Doreen poked at it with her chopsticks and laughed. "Mom, do you remember asking that cute server about the duck? You sounded interested, even nodded. I think we have a language problem here."

Marion covered her mouth with the linen napkin and laughed. "Yes, I must have confused her, poor girl."

No server was in the area of their table, so Doreen raised her hand to her lips and went to the restaurant's captain. He laughed, too, and promised salmon Sashimi would be delivered to their table in minutes. It was. Doreen said a silent prayer of thanks.

"So," Mom said, "what is your biggest concern

about the wedding?"

~

The two women hugged, two mothers who loved. Vivian set her tea cup down on the flowered saucer and rested her hand on Marion's. Marion gently placed her hand on Vivian's and smiled. "I am so glad you will be nearby to help Doreen."

Doreen noticed Mom's voice was shaky.

"Only if asked," Vivian said firmly.

Marion smiled again. "Thanks." But her voice was still wobbly.

Doreen had chosen the Café Jardin in the Sherman Foundation Gardens for lunch. It was such a beautiful and calming place with all the colorful flowers blooming. She had planned to show her mom the little rose garden where Noelle and Braydon had married, where he was the rose expert. But suddenly Mom rose and tossed her folded napkin next her plate.

"So much to do, Doreen. We need to get going. Thanks for lunch, Vivian."

Doreen nodded to Vivian and whispered a thank you for abandoning her at the table. What had happened here? She led Mom to her Lexus, seated her in the passenger side and burst into tears.

"What's wrong? What did I do?" Marion sounded contrite. She jutted her chin out and sat ramrod straight in her seat. Buckling her seatbelt she turned to Doreen.

"She's a nice woman. I just don't want her to take over your life."

~

Mom was jealous. Her sweet mother who never

got angry or gossiped, the one who prayed for others. The mother who swore she'd never mistrust Doreen. Time to call Melanie.

"Mel," Doreen took a cleansing breath and almost laughed remembering how she collapsed on the floor of her closet when she and Connie did one in tandem. But Mel didn't know about that, so the whooshing sound obviously worried her.

"Doreen, is that you? What's wrong. You're scaring me."

"Mom's in a snit."

"What's she doing?"

"She is behaving very weird for her."

"Weird how?" Doreen could almost see Melanie squinting her eyes. Maybe scratching her nose, too.

Doreen told Mel about the incident at Sherman Gardens, how her mom tossed her napkin on the table and barely acknowledged Vivian.

"She also said she's afraid of losing me to Vivian. How can that be?"

"Mmm. That's the way my mom acted when she was having marital trouble with that horrible man Bruce." Doreen heard a long silence. "Maybe I shouldn't have said that. Do you think everything is okay with your parents?" She obviously avoided asking about their marriage.

~

The first thing Doreen concluded was that Mom was lonely. But why? Since Dad retired they had more time to spend together going to dinner out, couples Bible study, and local fun events. Retirement was supposed to be a gift after years of working, wasn't it?

She remembered a few conversations she'd had with Mom recently. When she asked what fun things they were doing the responses were standard, void of emotion. She's assumed Mom was tired after a long day of fun.

"We went to another couples group last night.

"The county fair is in town. Nice to see the pigs and animals again.

"Dinner at the Pancake Palace was good, as usual. Dad had his standard breakfast for dinner, I had the senior pot roast meal."

Doreen rubbed her forehead and sat down on the bench in her bedroom. Those comments did lack enthusiasm. They'd waited so long for their retirement years. Were her parents in a slump?

Thirteen

Doreen awakened to the smell of coffee, vanilla, and caramel. Yum! She threw on a robe and staggered into the kitchen. Mom was scrambling eggs, sausage was frying in a copper pan. A much better treat than her usual yogurt.

Mom turned and a smile lit up her face. "Hope this is okay. I like my usual breakfast."

"Oh, Mom, it's lovely." Doreen wrinkled her nose and sniffed the lovely aromas. "I don't often make this kind of breakfast for myself. Thank you."

"You need to stay healthy with all the demands on your schedule." Marion turned Doreen by the shoulders to look her in the eyes. "Is Connie putting too much pressure on you?"

Doreen sank into a chair at the breakfast table, wiped both hands across her eyes, and laughed so loud she startled her mom.

"What? She is?"

"No, Mom. This situation managing the boutique is a gift. So is the modeling." She raised her eyes to focus on her mother's. "Do you not understand how blessed I am?"

Fourteen

Bill tossed the phone. It landed on the kitchen counter with a thud and skittered, almost dropping in the sink. He looked at his hand, still shaking. What had happened here?

He'd assumed. What was that old phrase? Yes, he was an ass. His knees got so weak when he'd heard her voice they wobbled. After tossing the phone he sat down hard on a chair. This couldn't be true. He knew it wasn't true.

Marina was syrupy sweet and malicious. Golden liquid dripped over the phone lines. How had he ever gotten involved with her? In fact, how did he know her? He tried to remember.

He had been only twenty-one, sent to Italy for a unique modeling assignment after the stint in Germany. Thrilled to be chosen and to make a lot of money. Dad had cautioned him to be wary, to be sure, to read the contract carefully. He thought he had. Then he met her.

She'd sat outside right after the contract

signing. Waiting, enticingly perched on a step. Her dark curls blew around her rosy cheeks and clung to her neck and her dazzling eyes were sky-blue like his. He remembered reading about how people with similar characteristics were attracted to each other. It was called mirroring. Like seeing yourself in another. When she'd lifted her hand toward his he grasped it and felt the promise of something magical.

Then she said, "Do you like my shoes?" She lifted a foot toward him, almost touching his nose. They were glittering silver, sparkling in the sun.

He was dazzled by her eyes and the shoes and her.

She'd led him to a loft. She'd started to carefully unbutton his shirt, and his body got cold. So cold it was almost like ice.

"What's wrong, Billy Boy? You scared?" Her laughter still rang in his ears.

He looked at the phone on the counter and sank to his knees.

~

Marina was lying. Was that even her name? He remembered the enticement of the open blouse down to her navel, the pursed lips, the flirtatious blinking eyes. Thankfully, he had held his ground, clung to his beliefs. He knew he hadn't succumbed to her ploys. He had made a vow and kept it. Even under the pressure of an Italian seductress.

Marina was evil. Was then, still now. But why now after so many years? Should he share with Doreen? How much would she understand? He rose from his knees. Trust. He needed trust, and he must trust.

He gazed into Doreen's hazel eyes. Tonight they were jade green. Was that a sign?

"She says you have a child? An eleven-year-old child?" Doreen tore the napkin into shreds. "How can that be?" She touched his hand. He didn't raise his eyes.

~

"Mom, what are you doing?"

"Packing."

"Why?"

"Time to leave. You don't need me here anymore. Vivian will help you plan."

Doreen looked at the small pile of carefully folded clothes her mother was arranging in the overnight bag. Such a waste of time and energy. They had planned to go to the shop tomorrow for mother of the bride gown ideas, something special Connie could create after knowing Marion's preferences.

"Mom, what about tomorrow?"

"What about it? I can find a nice dress in Montana. No need to trouble yourself on my account. Vivian will look like a model in one of Connie's creations. I am content to look like me."

Doreen flung the gift card at her mother's suitcase. "Here is the appointment for your gown. Compliments of Connie." She stormed out of the room. "You decide if you want a gown designed by a renowned designer for my wedding. Up to you."

Fifteen

"I want to meet her. I want to see pictures of the child." Doreen crossed her arms, leaned them on their favorite Starbucks table and narrowed her eyes staring into Bill's. She wanted what she called determined confirmation. A silly phrase she had conjured up after her surgery and recovery, but one she clung to now in this devastating situation.

Bill wiped his brow with a beige paper napkin. "I don't think that's a good idea."

"I insist." She glared at him. "This is my future and yours. Ours." When he didn't look up and crumpled the napkin, she rose and walked out.

"Damn, I stumbled. Need more faith, Lord. Sorry." She teetered uncertainly to her car rocking on the stiletto heels she had worn to impress him, opened the door with care and slid into the driver's seat. She flung her purse on the passenger seat, clicked the seat belt, and collapsed against the wheel, heaving in wracking sobs.

~

Natalie picked up the phone and answered without waiting. "What does it matter if you can't dance? How important is that? Can you fake it?"

The sobbing and hiccupping finally computed. "Oh, my gosh, Dor. What's wrong?"

"He . . . he had an affair. He might have an eleven-year-old child. In Italy."

"Coming right over." Nat grabbed her keys, slipped her feet into her flops and raced to the door.

She pulled into the curved drive in front of Doreen's townhome and slammed on the brakes causing her little car to lurch. "Gotta remember to stop before putting into park," she admonished herself. "Time for maintenance." The message on her dashboard said 35 Days Overdue For Service A1.'"

Doreen pulled the door open and collapsed against it. Nat grabbed her wrist and led her to the sofa. "Calling Melanie," she said as she punched numbers on her cellphone. Doreen only nodded with tears streaming down her face.

Sixteen

Melanie burst into the room without ringing the bell and flung herself on Doreen's other side from the one Natalie was pressed against. The two friends held Doreen tight and rocked her. Finally, the wracking sobs turned to sniffles.

Passing her a tissue, Melanie said, "Okay. Tell all. Now!" she demanded and thrust another tissue in Doreen's hand. "Blow."

Doreen hugged her arms. "He denies it, but this woman, Marina is her name, insists."

"Go on," Nat said rubbing the arm next to her. "What makes her so sure?"

"She swears she had an affair with him. After one of his photo shoots for Ducati. He swears he didn't." She gulped. "Who should I believe?"

~

The three friends were sipping mugs of herb tea when Noelle burst in. "I just heard."

"How?"

"The Candy Cane grapevine is phenomenal,"

she quipped. "Actually, it had something to do with Dor's mom not wanting Connie to design her MOB gown, which led to a conversation with Vivian who called Candy who called me." She paused to catch a breath and cradle her almost nine-month-old pregnant belly. "Got it?"

"Where is your mom?" Melanie asked Doreen.

"She took a Lyft to the mall while I was at work. Thank goodness she's not here to see me in this blubbering state."

"You okay being here?" Nat asked Noelle. "You don't have to be. We got this under control."

"I want to be, need to be, after all the abuse I dealt with from Clay and Bruce, your stepfather, Mel. Sorry. Part of my history. Wanna help."

"So, what is your wisdom, Noelle?" Melanie was grateful for her help, but her past problems were so different from Doreen's.

"I want to lend some perspective. And advice."

Doreen nodded. "Please."

"First do not jump to conclusions. You weren't there. You don't really know what happened. Maybe Bill doesn't either."

"You don't think he could have been lying?" Doreen asked hopefully.

"Do you trust him? Has he ever lied about anything else?" Noelle grasped Doreen's hands and squeezed. Doreen shook her head. "Never."

"Call Big Bill. I bet your Bill already called him." She lowered herself carefully into the soft chair still hugging her belly.

~

Vivian answered the phone. So unusual. Where

was Bill? Doreen's damp hands gripped her phone so tightly they almost slipped.

"Hello, dear." Vivian's voice was soft. "I know. It's going to be okay. God gave me a sign."

"What kind of sign?"

"A butterfly. The one He always gives me when I'm troubled. Very clear sign. The delicate butterfly hovers near my favorite potted plant right outside my kitchen door. She, I know it's a she, tastes the alyssum, turns toward me, then flutters away." Vivian sighed into the phone. "She is my little angel."

"Here's Bill," she said suddenly. She must have handed the phone off to him. His booming voice took over.

"Doreen? Doreen? Are you okay?"

"I am better now."

"I hope so. Let's get this straight." Doreen held the phone away from her ear so the other girls could hear. Hardly necessary, though, because Bill's voice resonated throughout the room.

"First, I do trust my son. Second, I do not trust this situation. Third, I am going to look into it." He paused, and the girls heard a slurping sound. Maybe he took take a sip of Vivian's tea? "I do not trust this Marina woman, nor the Ducati company. Was never sure about them, not totally comfortable sending Billy off to Italy to model for them. But he was so young and so excited. I didn't want to deprive him. Water under many bridges at this point."

Doreen thanked Big Bill and clicked off the phone with a sigh. "Maybe I am overreacting, not trusting enough."

"I don't think you can overreact in a situation like this," Candy stated bluntly as she burst into the room.

"Oh, my gosh, you, too? I am overcome with love and support." She clung to Candy's outstretched hand. "What do you think I should do?"

"First things, first. I'm sure you girls have already prayed, but I want to be part of that. We need to be audacious, bold, send our requests supernaturally to heaven."

The women clasped hands. Noelle began. "Dear Heavenly Father . . . Oh, Oooo!"

The others clasped hands tighter. Why did Noelle stop? Natalie opened her eyes to peek.

"Oooo is right! Somebody call Braydon. Somebody get towels to mop up the floor. You, Melanie and Candy, guide Noelle to someone's car. With towels," she added.

Seventeen

"Who are all of you?" The charge nurse Rita's eyes swept over more people than she'd ever remembered waiting for an impending birth. A very unusual group.

"We are Noelle's family, her extended, loving family," Melanie announced.

"Mmm. Very unusual." They heard Nurse Rita mumble under her breath. "But I guess okay. As long as you stay here in the guest area. And, please keep quiet."

Her shoulders quivered as she walked away.

"I think she has our number," Natalie quipped.

"She was actually nice," Doreen said.

"Why am I here?" Bill, Jr. asked.

"Don't question," Big Bill said with authority.

Vivian had been quiet, sitting off to the side. Standing up and spreading her hands she whispered. Her grayish hair fluttered from the whir of the air conditioning units, but her eyes were clear as she swept her gaze around the group. Her lips moved slightly. She seemed to be counting them. Doreen, Melanie, Natalie, Candy, Bill, Jr. and Big Bill. Herself, too. Just then Darrel and Kerstin Day and Logan and Lydia Lovejoy quietly took seats. Vivian looked around and made eye contact with each of the newcomers. As she was about to say a comforting prayer another silent person slipped in. What was Marion Zimmer doing here? She welcomed her with an air kiss then began to pray.

Just as "Amen" passed Vivian's lips they heard an ear-splitting cry. Then a chiming bell. A baby is born. Braydon had pushed the announcement bell. A privilege for fathers of newborn
babies.

Everyone cheered. Some cried, but most smiled and grinned. The Candy Canes had a new baby.

Connie and Cindy screamed from their cellphones, too far away in Scottsdale and Costa Rica to be present. But in Newport Beach in heart.

"I want to know all," Connie cried in frustration. "Weight, length, everything. Please."

Vivian started a group call on the sophisticated cellphone Bill had bought her, the one he still didn't know how to use. She chuckled to herself about his lack of technology. Still, she felt compelled to share. Thankfully all had gone well with little Braydon Logan Darrell Lovejoy.

"Wow, what a handle," Vivian exclaimed as she was punching numbers with her shaking fingers.

"Two at a time," Nurse Rita said firmly. "The parents want to see you, but only two at a time."

Cellphone cameras flashed and cries of excitement mixed with baby sounds. After the two sets of beaming grandparents came out of the birthing room, Melanie and Natalie were next. Vivian and Big Bill finally got their turn. Doreen and Candy were last.

Bill, Jr. declined with a mumbled, "Don't need me."

Doreen looked at him oddly. Did he mean Noelle and Braydon didn't need to see him, or was he making an excuse because of embarrassment? Or because of the idea of a baby since being confronted by Marina? She decided to let it go. After all she couldn't control his emotions.

Finally, Cindy and Connie got photos and stats, 19 inches, 7 pounds, and a head of blonde hair. Their squealing could be heard all along the hospital hallway. Nurses laughed and high-fived each other.

Eighteen

Doreen, Melanie and Natalie collapsed on Doreen's sofa. Marion had come back with them in Doreen's car, then excused herself and went to her bedroom. The girls all looked and felt disheveled, and were definitely tired. Melanie wiped her brow and Nat dabbed at her eyes after grabbing a tissue from the side table. Doreen kicked off her shoes to wiggle her toes.

The sun was trying to set, its brilliant hues of orange and fuchsia glared through her living room window. Although her condo was several miles from the Pacific, she was sure she heard the seagulls' cries. Maybe it was her imagination, or a text on her phone. She crossed her longer right leg over the left one, reached for the phone on the coffee table, and clicked it off. Billy would have to wait.

"I guess tonight put life in perspective," she mumbled.

"What did you say, Dor?" Mel wiped her

forehead again.

"She said tonight gave us hope," Nat responded.

Doreen nodded and stood for a moment to stare out the window, then picked up her tossed- off shoes. Dangling them from one hand, she retreated to her bedroom.

"Should we go after her?" Nat asked.

"No. Leave her alone for a while. She needs peace."

No one knew more than Melanie how much peace Doreen needed. She had caused the accident that Doreen had suffered with during almost six hours of surgery ending in a shortened leg, plus weeks of infection, so Melanie knew the need for peace. No only had she, Melanie, lost a baby, but a husband. She was so thankful to her Candy Cane sisters who prayed for her and guided her to Jesus. She clung to them and to the Holy Spirit for guidance. She prayed for Doreen now. She believed all would be okay for her, but she felt she needed human confirmation.

"Hi, Bill! How are you doing?"

Although she couldn't see him, she almost believed his hand was on the back of his neck. Hadn't Doreen said he did that when he was nervous?

"Hi. Mel, I think? That you?"

"Yep, me." She waited for more. When it didn't come, she thrust ahead.

Nineteen

Bill was uncomfortable with Melanie's questions. He knew she and Doreen were close, but wasn't the situation with Marina private? His and Doreen's alone? He decided to be honest.

"Uh, Melanie, this is private between Dor and me." Did she understand?

"Sorry, Bill, but Nat and I have spent hours with her sobbing. If we are going to help her, and you," she added, "we need more information. So, spill, Bill, spill." Melanie couldn't believe she had been so confrontational with Bill, but she was very worried about her friend.

Bill grumbled but told her the whole wretched story that Marina had flung in his face. "I know I didn't do anything with her."

"I know Doreen trusts you, but you need to be sure. Where is this child she says you fathered? Is he here in the U.S.? How about a DNA test to confirm you are not his father?" Maybe she had gone too far, but she was so worried about Dor and

Bill's relationship. It was no longer a secret. She never heard Bill's answer. She heard Bill click the button on his phone. Was he sobbing?

~

Bill had read the book *Why bad things happen to good people*, or something like that. But he never thought anything this awful would happen to him. Time to call Dad again.

"Aw, ha! Wondered when you'd call." Big Bill heard only silence on his end. Then, he questioned if silence can be heard. He laughed.

Of course, Billy thought, Vivian the ultimate prayer warrior and advisor would get on the phone. Dad always passed it to her during difficult conversations. But not tonight.

"If it's true, you must step up to the plate. If it's not, you must find out." Dad sighed, not a usual response from him. "Sadly, Bill, I think you must insist on a DNA test. I hope the child is here where it can be done."

When Bill hung up, he felt better, but not completely. Dad hadn't said he believed him. Did he?

How would he get the deceptive Marina to comply? In almost all countries, the mother's wishes took precedence, especially in European countries. He would have to try.

And pray.

Twenty

Doreen felt better, more under control. The Candy Cane sisters had helped with prayers and suggestions. Bill had texted her last night.

It's going to be okay. We will work it out.

Such a guy response. Whatever.

She slipped in the rear door to Winning Designs, reset the security device, put her purse in the back room, opened the shades, and stood ready to push the button to unlock the main door. Who was scheduled to come in for fittings today? Yesterday she had brought up the request from Rita Spaulding. Wow, the wonderful nurse on the birthing unit at the hospital when Noelle and Braydon gave birth to their adorable little son with the impossibly long name. Apparently, the new norm for male baby names included both grandfathers. An honor, or a way to be included in the wills?

It was barely ten a.m. Few Newport socialites seldom came that early, but Rita Spaulding did.

"Am I on time?" the soft voice asked. "I need to be at work by eleven."

Doreen clasped her hands. "I am thrilled you will allow me to help you chose your gown. When is the wedding?'

"Mmm, not for almost a year. Ten months actually. But I want to get started." She grinned at Doreen. "Nurses have schedules. We have to be on point."

Doreen asked all the expected questions. Where, when, what kind of ceremony, how large, how many attendants, what is your dream wedding?

Doreen hugged Rita Spaulding. It was so nice to help a real person, not a diva. The woman was so excited about her wedding to Kent her fiancé. She actually wanted it to be in the hospital where she worked, just like Melanie's in Scottsdale. Not the same hospital, but the one where Rita worked in Newport Beach.

Doreen thought about that. Could she help make it happen?

She punched some buttons on her cellphone. She was sure Connie would support her idea.

"Of course, Dor. I love to help. What do you suggest?"

"Obviously her gown. I didn't make a big deal about price, wanted her to love the gown. Maybe I went over the top."

She heard the Connie sigh. Then . . . "It's okay. I agree. This woman is special, needs a special situation."

"So," Connie said, "What is happening with your difficult situation?"

"Tell you later, Con. Bell just rang." The two friends hung up.

The inventory was so high-end that customers had to ring a bell to be invited into the boutique much like a jewelry store. Even the samples were extremely expensive. No more than two patrons could come in at a time. Connie had learned the hard way when she allowed several women in at once. A bride-to-be could bring all her attendants at the same time, even her mother and the MOG, Mother of the Groom, and the flower girls. But only one bride's group was allowed in at a time. That's why appointments were a necessity after that random girl stuffed a twenty-five hundred-dollar gown under her flowing caftan. Fortunately, Connie realized a gown was missing within five minutes. She'd reported it to the Newport Beach Police giving what she thought was an accurate description. Gratefully, the wonderful police force, especially Sargent Gilroy, apprehended the thief within an hour. Now every serious client accepted the requirement. In fact, they all loved it because it was like a private showing.

Doreen spoke into the bell speaker. "Hello. Do you have an appointment?"

Hesitation. "I, uh, not know I need one."

"Are you looking for a gown? For a special occasion?"

"Yes, for weedding, my weedding. My amica, friend," she seemed to correct herself, "recommend shop to me. Say go to this shop." She paused. "I not from here. I not know rules. Not know neeed appointament. I try not to bee too long," the woman babbled on. But she appeared to be having trouble expressing herself.

"I see. I don't have another appointment for forty-five minutes. So come in, please." She clicked the button to release the lock on the door. *The woman sounded very nervous. Lots of clients are, so why wonder about this one? Why am I curious? The difficulty speaking English? But I have many foreign clients who stumble over words.*

Doreen extended her hand to the slender, dark-haired woman and clasped it warmly. "Welcome to Winning Designs."

The petite woman, almost a foot shorter than her, nodded and giggled. There was something strange about her luxurious raven hair that clung to her shoulders in curls. Aha, no part! Odd.

The woman giggled again. *Must be extra nervous.*

"I'm Doreen, the shop curator. You are?"

"Reena." She emphasized the last letter of her name, lilting it.

"May I have your last name?" Doreen almost giggled asking that silly question, but all clients had to be recorded, especially after Connie's bad experience. "I hope you understand we keep track of all our clients. Especially the brides. It's really a formality so we can accommodate you in the future with modifications and changes." She handed the woman a printed form and a pen with a silk rose adorning it. Pulling out a chair by the antique writing desk, she gestured to Rina.

"Ees necessary to look at gowns? To see eef I like?" Doreen noticed Rina spoke slowly and deliberately as if making sure her English pronunciation was correct. But there was still an accent. She couldn't decipher it, maybe some difficulty in expressing herself and pronouncing pronouns.

"I'll be glad to fill out the form for you. I can ask questions. Would that help?" The woman shrugged her shoulders.

"Maybe if you told me your wedding date? And, of course, your last name and fiancé's name. All important stuff." She tried to be casual and make the woman feel comfortable.

The woman spun on her heel. She had never sat down. What was she afraid of?

"I think ees wrong place for mee. Sorry I bother you." She raced the short distance to the front door and tried to tug it open.

"Are you sure? I'd love to help you."

"Why I cannot get out? Oh, da bell ting."

Doreen buzzed her out and the normally silent door almost slammed. Such a sad experience, one she'd never had before in the boutique. Several times she'd had to guide brides-to-be to other venues, even offered advice. It was always sad to prick a balloon for their dreams. But she had to be honest. Connie's designs were extravagant and very expensive. She knew in her heart that many brides would find lovely gowns they could afford at David's Bridal. One former bride who couldn't afford Winning Designs came back to thank her. "You may not believe this, but you gave me the best advice ever. I found my dream gown at Ross for Less in exactly my size! Thank you so much for being caring and honest."

Doreen and Connie were thrilled to hear this. That's what the boutique was really about. Chasing dreams.

Doreen pondered about the strange woman, mostly her behavior. She'd seemed frightened. She never told her a last name, nor where she was from. Then it struck her.

Twenty-one

"Con? Connie, are you there?"

"Sorry. Was changing a diaper. What's up?

Doreen was sure her sigh could be heard across two states from California to Arizona. "Not sure, but I think Bill's woman who is accusing him came into the shop today."

"What! On what pretense?"

Doreen told her the situation and how the woman scooted away after trying to get her to register as a client.

"Sounds like she was scared."

"I think so, too. But, why did she come?"

"To see you. Obviously, Dor. Wanted to know what she was up against." Connie chuckled.

"Please don't laugh, Con. This is serious. I am scared."

"Doreen, I think, no believe, you should go ahead with your wedding plans to Bill. I feel strongly about it. What do Melanie and Natalie say?"

"Haven't told them about today."

~

Doreen called Bill. "Would she do that?" she asked. "Did you tell her where I work? My name?"

Long silence. Then, "Must have uh mentioned both. But," he continued, "why would she? Doesn't make sense."

Doreen would have slapped him if she could. Men! So totally clueless. She tried to calm herself and keep her voice low-keyed. Did she need to walk him through Romance 101?

She whooshed out a cleansing breath, her new calming method, and finally said, "Billy, I think it's time to call Vivian and your dad for advice." She hung up the phone quietly and took a shower.

~

"What?" Vivian almost screamed – so unlike her. "She actually had the . . ." several inappropriate phrases almost came across. She was obviously very angry. Finally, she whispered "the nerve."

Doreen almost laughed, would have if she wasn't so nervous herself and strung out. "Yes, Vivian, she did. I know it was her. She refused to register, she was tiny and had a Mediterranean appearance, her English was perfect except for a few words, and she looked me up and down. Like deciding on a special sale item in the grocery store, or Walmart. Ugh!"

Vivian passed the phone to Big Bill as usual.

"What the rudgyfudgy is going on?" Doreen remembered he loved to use that made-up word to cover the swear words he wanted to say. She almost gave in to another laugh. Her future in laws were a hoot. She was blessed.

~

"Yes, Dor, you are blessed," Nat said. Why was Doreen even questioning? "I have an idea. I can take off a few hours at the gym and come to the boutique to help you. It would be fun for me. You okay with that?"

"I would love that, Nat. Tomorrow?"

"Ten sharp. Buzz me in," she added with a chuckle.

Doreen's other call was from Melanie. "I got you, girl. I am coming over right now."

Doreen pulled open the door just as Melanie's foot crossed the threshold. They collapsed in each other's arms and sank on the sofa. Mom was in the guest bathroom taking a shower.

"Gotta do something proactive," Mel said.

"What? You have an idea?"

"I'm not too good at this, but I think you need to Google her. Even do an ancestry exploration. Maybe there's something that says she's done this before." Mel paused and Doreen could almost see the wheels turning under Mel's long brown hair.

"What about Googling the child?"

"That seems like a weird idea, Mel. Would there be information on a child?"

"Or," Mel continued, "the family. What is her surname?"

"Capelli, Bill said. Pretty common, I think."

"So, let's try." She pulled up Doreen's laptop and started punching in.

"Says here on Google that Capelli means hair, and 'of the chapel.' Also angel hair pasta."

"That's my favorite. With only tomatoes and black olives. I will never order that again!"

"Don't be silly, Dor. It's just a Google explanation of the name."

Twenty-two

Doreen collapsed with clothes on and wrapped the down comforter around her shaking body. What was going on here? What had suddenly come between her and Billy? She couldn't believe he was lying. Could he have had a lapse in memory because of something? Drugs the woman had administered to him? Being exhausted from the photo shoots? Or just plain lying? But on whose part?

She turned over hoping to succumb to sleep. Maybe she should get a dog. Like Mel and Connie and Jaeda. Dogs gave comfort, didn't they? She would call Melanie in the morning.

~

"Of course you should get a dog!" Melanie said. "My sweet Lola is the best companion ever. Got me through that trauma with Francine, Larry's supposed mother."

Doreen thought about that horrible time when homeless Francine stalked Melanie and how Bill and Vivian had taken the woman in.

"What happened? I know Big Bill and Vivian took her in, but . . .?"

"She found the Lord. And a boyfriend. The delivery man. She is now their so-called housekeeper with her little dog Sam." Melanie chuckled. "The man who brought Sam to her. Cute, huh?"

"Does she still claim to be your mother-in-law, Larry's mother?" Doreen lowered her chin. "Sorry. That was insensitive of me bringing Larry up. How are you about him, now?"

"I'm okay, Dor. It's been hard. But, I did, and still do, love him very much. He did a lot wrong, a lot illegally, but he gave me back my self-confidence as a woman. I am still working through it, especially with my friend Robert from the grief group. Who has his own problems." Melanie laughed. "Francine is really a dear. I'm glad she is in my life. We've never done a DNA test, but I don't want to. I believe in my heart she really is Larry's mother. We have worked it out. With, of course, Bill and Vivian's help and prayers.

"Now, back to adopting."

Doreen hugged Mel, so glad for their friendship. After tears, she answered Doreen's question.

"But what about leaving it alone for hours?"

"Easy. Take it out in the morning, give lots of treats and love, come back after work and more treats and love. Take out to your yard for a brief peeing and pooping, then cuddle."

"Sounds so simple."

"Dor, you are still a stress case. This is simple. Not rocket science. Just love shared."

Mel pressed on. "Think about how little Jake brought Connie and Jaeda together, even helped her during her pregnancy. That is the best story I know."

Doreen remembered. She was sure they all did. If it hadn't been for Connie tripping over Jake several times the doctor wouldn't have prescribed physical therapy for her at Spine Scottsdale, and Emily Sullivan, Shane's wife, wouldn't have picked up on the fact Connie was pregnant with twins. God works in mysterious ways. What would He do for her?

"Will you go with me?"

"To adopt? Yes, but only if you adopt. Not if you want to have a purebred from a breeder."

"I don't want some fussy little dog who was bred for a lot of money. I want a dog who wants me."

"Can you take Saturday off?"

"Nat is coming in to help. Maybe I can."

~

"Why are all those dogs barking?"

"Because they want your attention, want to be adopted." Melanie grabbed her elbow and pulled. "Come on." She registered with the receptionist and a sweet older lady beckoned them. After introducing herself, Adelaide led them forward.

"Do you have a particular breed or kind or size of dog in mind?" she asked.

Doreen shook her head. "Just a sweet companion. And one I can leave alone while I work."

"Maybe a smaller dog would be best for you."

"I need a cuddler."

Adelaide raised her brows and smiled.

The threesome walked by kennels, all with adoptable dogs. Some sad-eyed, some jumping for attention, some cowering in the back of cages.

"I can't do this!" Doreen turned to walk away covering her eyes. "Too sad."

"Maybe," Adelaide said, "we are going this all wrong." She paused and looked Doreen in the eyes. "What is your home like? Stuffed sofas? Contemporary furniture? Do you have a yard? Tell me your daily schedule. How do you feel about sharing your bed with a pet? Are there windows a pet can look out of with walking traffic? But mostly, tell me why you are here?"

Melanie started to answer for her. "She's going through a rough patch right now. She . . ."

"I'm having some personal problems. But," she added, "I have a deep faith and am surrounded by friends, friends of faith. I need something stable in my life, a constant, dependable. Someone to come home to. Someone who doesn't care what I look like, or even how I smell after a long day." The other two women chuckled at that remark. "Melanie here has an adorable dog Lola, and another dear friend has Jake, a Miniature Pinscher."

Adelaide's eyes lit up. "This may be a silly, off the wall question," she hesitated, "but any chance that little Min-Pin dog was a model?" She started to shake her head. "No, no. Sorry. Silly of me."

Doreen and Melanie burst out laughing. "You

know? You saw Jake in magazine ads?"

"With his owner, a tall handsome black dude. Oh, my goodness! You are the other model. Right?" Her face flushed, but she prattled on. "So embarrassed. I remember reading your story in the newspaper, how you were injured, how you became a model for women with disabilities." She reached out both hands to clasp Doreen's. "I heard you forgave the person who caused your accident?" It was a question. One Doreen was delighted to answer. She lifted Melanie's hand.

"Yes, I did. This is that person. Now my best friend."

Adelaide's eyes pooled, and she tugged a tissue out of the Kleenex box on the counter to wipe them. "I didn't mean to get so personal. But I am honored," Adelaide said. Turning away quickly, she announced, "I will bring a dog out for you to meet and visit with. Okay?"

Doreen and Mel nodded, tears tickling their lashes, too. They sat down on the hard chairs. Within minutes Adelaide stood before them with a small, fluffy dog in her arms.

"This is Happy Arthur," she said as she placed the bundle of fur in Doreen's arms. "He is very loyal, but he does need daily brushing and an occasional bath. In your tub or even your sink since he is so small."

"Does he know any commands? I know some dogs understand sit, stay, and down."

"Actually," the woman said smiling, "he does. Not sure why because of where we found him. Maybe the foster mom taught him."

"Why is he here? What happened?"

"Uh," she looked away and hesitated.

"Please tell me. Was he abused?"

"No. Not actually abused. Abandoned."

"I'm not supposed to share all this, but since you and Arthur seem to like each other . . ." she smiled again as Arthur licked Doreen's chin and Doreen snuggled close to his furry face.

"He was found in a scrap yard with a horrible burn across his little back." She looked at Doreen in a funny way. Maybe hoping his injuries wouldn't scare her and she wouldn't change her mind about him.

"Tell me more, please." Doreen's voice trembled.

"His foster mom said it looked as if he'd crawled under a car and hot oil dripped on him." She hesitated. "They kept him for six months to be sure his back was healed. He was only a puppy when they found him. He's a survivor."

"Tell me, please, about the foster family."

"I honestly don't know much. I remember they had two little girls. I do have contact information. I promised to let them know about Happy."

"I want to belong to Happy Arthur." Doreen grinned with moist eyes. "But, part of the deal is I want to be in contact with the family. I want any children to know he is loved and cared for. Deal?"

~

"You are such a crazy softie." Mel squeezed Dor's hand, the one that wasn't holding Arthur's leash. He didn't tug, just pranced obediently beside Doreen. What a gift!

"Those people need to know this dog is loved and cared for. I will do that, thanks to Adelaide bending the rules. I will email the family tonight."

She scooped Happy Arthur into her arms, snuggled her face in his whiskers and twirled around.

"Look, Mel, he's almost dancing.

"I have an idea! I will practice dancing with him. Maybe he will give me the confidence to dance."

She almost forgot about the Billy situation and Rina, and the boy.

Almost.

BONNIE ENGSTROM

Twenty-three

"What happened today?" Doreen held the phone to her ear. She was concerned, even worried, about Winning Designs and Natalie taking her place. She had to call to find out.

"It was fine, Dor. You need to relax and have faith. I did okay. Really. What did you do today?"

"I adopted a dog!"

"Wow! That's great. Tell me."

"His name is Arthur. He's an adorable little fluffy thing I will have to brush every day. That," she said with emphasis, "will keep me busy."

"I hope it will keep your mind off of . . ." She couldn't finish the comment, but Doreen knew what she meant.

"Did you learn any more? I know you and Mel Googled."

"Not a whole lot. But we learned Capelli is an old Venetian name, or at least from the north of Italy. Doesn't tell us much."

"But," Natalie pressed on, "did you Google her

name? Maybe something will show up."
"We are doing that now. We'll let you know."

"Please send a photo of Arthur. I'm dying to meet him."

"Sure. After having worked at the shop today, anything to report?"

"Not too much. Mrs. Ingle came in with her daughter. An appointment you'd booked."

"What were they like? I've never met them. But she is a big time volunteer for cancer research and homeless kids."

"Very nice lady. Daughter, too. Money was no option."

"Did daughter choose a gown?"

"Not yet, but tried on twenty plus." Natalie laughed, her deep chuckle so familiar.

Doreen thanked Nat and said she would be back to work in the morning after church.

~

She'd decided to enter by the front door to make sure the signs in the window were in place. She was punching in her security code when she felt a presence behind her. Not exactly threatening, but warm breath on her neck. Doreen spun around and almost collided with the other woman.

"Ees too eerly?"

Doreen quickly scoped the woman. Fiftyish, carried a Louis Viton purse hanging from a manicured hand, nails bright blue. Long dark hair so perfectly coiffured it had been done less than an hour ago. Probably by Robert. She would call him later to find out. The light breeze ruffled Doreen's chin length hair, but the other woman's didn't move. Too much hair spray? Not Robert's style, and he didn't work on Sundays. The large eyes in her heart-shaped face looked terrified. Not like a prima donna there for a standard appointment.

Doreen extended her hand and was rewarded with a limp damp one. Who is this woman, and what does she want?

She asked the woman's name hoping it was on the roster, and with an appointment she didn't remember.

"Naomi Capelli." It was barely a whisper.

Capelli? Can't be a coincidence. Could it?

Doreen unlocked the door and led the woman inside. "Please have a seat. I would appreciate it if you started to fill out the form." She handed her one, and the woman looked at her blankly.

"A form? Why I haf fill out form to shop?"

After explaining this was a private shop with dedicated customers, and hoping she would be one, Doreen smiled her brightest.

"So glad you found us," Doreen said with fake enthusiasm. "I am here to help. Are you looking for a mother of the bride or groom gown? Or for the bride?"

She hadn't expected an honest answer, but she was startled at the woman's reaction.

The so-called Capelli woman shoved back the padded chair and flung the form on the floor. Still trying to be gracious, Doreen bent to retrieve the paper and noticed the woman's shoes. Manolo Blahnik! At least $2000 a pair. By the designer who has four factories in Italy, who was born to wear a cape, the man who is petulant and eccentric in several languages. That was what Doreen had once read about the mysterious designer. But even as a top model, she had never worn his shoes.

Before she could try to engage the Capelli woman again she was banging on the door.

"Let mee out!"

Doreen was attempted to say, "Not until you tell me who you are and why you're here." But good breeding took over, and she pushed the door buzzer. The Winning Designs door didn't slam, but the whoosh was obvious.

Twenty-four

"I've decided to call him Happy because I am so happy to have him, and he seems happy to be with me. His formal name will be Happy Arthur. What do you think?" Doreen posed the question to Melanie who nodded.

"I think it's perfect. Your call, Dor." She gave a wide grin and reached for a cuddle.

"Another weird woman today in Winning Designs. Another Capelli. How is that possible?"

Doreen was distraught. Thankfully Happy was here to help. He licked her chin, and Melanie could swear he grinned.

"Who are these people? How did they suddenly appear to spoil my future with Bill?" She looked to Melanie for answers. But Mel only shook her head and shrugged her shoulders.

"I thought we had a fairytale romance. The crippled girl and the handsome model." Wiping her eyes and chin where Happy had licked it, she burst into tears. "I guess not."

"I wish I were a better biblical scholar, Dor, but I do believe the closer one gets to the Lord, the more the evil one attacks. My Nana said that."

"I know. One of the women on my prayer chain told me that years ago. I sort of sluffed it off, but I do believe it . . . now."

Melanie hesitated. "I have recently read in several of my morning devotions about being courageous in prayer."

"Go on."

"Joyce Meyers and Christine Caine encourage it. Cindy Trimm really does. But Steven Furtick makes a big point about bold prayer, praying for our heart's desire and God's will with confidence, even audaciously. No holding back. Maybe that's what Candy was trying to tell us."

Doreen reached for Melanie's hand. "Let's pray that way."

"Let's call the others." Doreen dialed the group number for all the Candy Canes. Happy licked her chin.

~

When she hung up she felt a peace. Candy had led the group in prayer, Connie and Jaeda chimed in as did Natalie, and Cindy and Rob from far away in Costa Rica. So much blessing. Noelle was changing little Braydon's diaper, but Braydon said a heartfelt prayer. Remembering how he'd prayed for her during her accident and surgery, she was so comforted. She knew God heard.

Next she called her mother who always seemed to be out shopping. The woman loved the Fashion Island mall. Especially Bloomingdales. Then she called Bill. Why was he last?

"Finally I hear from you. I've been afraid to call. Scared actually. What's up?"

"What do you mean? Afraid to call. Why?"

"The wedding coordinator from the Back Bay venue, and the one from the Fashion Island Hotel, called me. I didn't know what to tell them. Do we have a date?"

Doreen pretended something on the stove needed attention and clicked off the phone. Was this man she planned to marry insensitive or just plain clueless? She called Braydon.

"I don't know Bill that well, Dor, but I don't think he's insensitive. I think he was truthful when he said he was scared to call you."

"That doesn't help, Bray. What should I do? You know the whole fabricated story about the eleven-year-old child. Need advice, friend."

"Un, hate to say this, but are you sure it is fabricated? Have you checked in any and all ways?"

"Melanie and I Googled the mother. Not much information, but she is iffy."

"Then I suggest you share the information with Bill and Google it together. Hopefully he can give insight. So sorry, Dor, but that's my best idea. You know I am praying."

"He wasn't much help," Doreen said when she disconnected.

"But you know Braydon's prayers soar right up to heaven," Melanie said.

"Time to call in the big gun, Big Bill."

This time Bill, Sr. did not put Vivian on. Instead he called his son.

He almost never swore, but during the group call Doreen and Melanie held their ears. Happy Arthur woofed.

Twenty-five

Why was Mom standing outside Doreen's condo? With her suitcase? Doreen slid her car into the driveway, not bothering to put it in the garage. Mom had said she was leaving tomorrow.

"What's going on, Mom?" Doreen touched her mother's shoulder.

"Told you I was going back home."

"But now? I thought tomorrow. So we could have a mom and daughter dinner tonight. Why are you out here?" She wrapped her arms around her mother and held tight.

"Waiting for the cab."

"Mom, this makes no sense. What is wrong?" Marion collapsed against Doreen sobbing.

Doreen led her inside and settled her on the sofa just as a cab pulled up. She stepped outside and waved it away. "Sorry. Mistake." The driver nodded with a smile, thankfully. Apparently, this had happened to him before.

"Now, Mom, let's get the whole story."

"Not sure how to explain. Or which part."

"Please share. I am your only child. I deserve to understand."

It took ten minutes and a lot of mumbling and tears. Finally, Marion spoke.

"I didn't know how to tell you. Especially when you are planning your wedding, the most important day of your life."

"No, Mom, the most important day of my life was the day I was born."

Marion looked at her with confusion. "You really mean that?"

"Of course, I do, and you and Dad are the most important people in my life."

"What about your Bill?"

"He is right up there as number three." Doreen laughed and hugged Mom. "But he doesn't define me as a person." When Mom looked at her questioningly, she nodded. "Yes, I believe we were meant for each other, but we are our own people. Always will be. Do you understand?"

Mom nodded and agreed to stay "for a while." No commitment how long. But Doreen hoped.

Doreen settled her mom in the guest room and covered her with the special quilt, the one Mom had made years ago for Doreen when she was in college. She brought the suitcase in from the porch, set it in the kitchen, and prayed.

The next morning Doreen started to crack the eggs, then stopped. Her mother was holding her chin in hands with elbows propped on the kitchen counter. Not a good sign.

"Throw on some clothes, Mom. Just sweats.

We are going out for breakfast. Simple, but a respite." Doreen laughed. "I'm not a good cook anyway. I just need to feed Happy Arthur and take him to the side yard."

Mom looked at her quizzically. "What's he doing with your shoe?"

The little white dog stood at Doreen's feet. One of her athletic shoes hung from his mouth. He cocked his head and shook the shoe like a rag toy. Doreen was sure he was smiling.

"Happy, what's up?" Doreen started to scold him but laughed instead. He wiggled away when she tried to rescue her shoe from him. With a growl and a tug he released the shoe and dropped it at her feet. Happy sighed and retreated to snuggle in his fancy bed by the door. Was he trying to tell her something? Melanie had said dogs were preceptive. What was Happy trying to tell her? She took the shoe back to her closet and set it next to its companion. The one Happy had brought her had wet, chewed up laces. Why had he chosen the left one with the insert?

Doreen and Mom settled in the car when the Bluetooth brought up Vivian's phone number. Now that California was hands free for cellphones, Doreen clicked the little phone icon on her dashboard.

Vivian's voice was clear and loud. Maybe too loud. Did she feel she needed to shout to be heard?

"Hi, Vivian. What's up, what's on your mind?"

"Getting right to the point," she chuckled. "Have you decided on your wedding venue?"

Doreen's arms went cold. How could she share

with her future mother-in-law, a woman she loved and trusted, but not with her own mother? She decided on the pass. She hated to be deceptive, but she wasn't ready to share. Not until she knew more why Mom was so upset.

"Not yet, Vivian. Sorry. Still working out details."

Vivian put down the phone and turned to Bill. "Something is wrong. Terribly wrong." Doreen and Marion could hear her before she clicked off, just before they pulled in to IHop.

~

"What the rudgy-fudgy is going on?" Big Bill's voice boomed as always.

Bill, Jr. rested the phone on the counter. He didn't need anything technical to know his dad was upset.

"I don't know, Dad. Do you?"

Big Bill sighed loudly, something he didn't do often. "From what Vivian says it sounds like the wedding may be off. Or," he added, "a major glitch. Is Doreen's mother the problem?"

Bill thought about that. Doreen had only introduced him to her mom briefly, and at Starbucks. No comfy family situation at Dor's townhome. "Not sure, Dad. Mrs. Zimmer seems a little aloof."

"Maybe she's worried about fitting in with the Newport crowd," Big Bill huffed. "Although Vivian and I are pretty low-keyed. I hope that's not it." Then came the afterthought, the one young Bill hoped to avoid. "Or," the thought was drawn out, "or, she's gotten wind of the Marina situation. Do you think Doreen told her?"

Bill wished he knew. Doreen had never said if she told her mom about the threat from Marina. He'd never asked. Why? Too scared? Probably. What was the use in pursuing it? Marina was obviously a stalker. He'd figured that out. He picked up his phone from the counter.

"Yes?" Big Bill's voice answered across the connection.

"I think it's time, Dad. Time to find out for sure."

"Give me the number she called you from."

~

"The senior breakfast, please." Marion fiddled with her napkin, then looked up at the server.

"Mom, you aren't a senior yet."

"It says 55 plus. I am definitely that."

"Guess so," Doreen snickered. "Have you talked with Dad? Is he okay alone?"

"Mrs. Murphy is checking in on him. She has brought him breakfast a couple of times. So I guess he's okay."

"Who is she? I don't remember you mentioning her."

Marion laughed. "She's our earthly angel. Lives next door."

It was so good to hear Mom laugh, so Doreen pressed on. "Why have you never told me about her? She sounds wonderful."

"Guess," Mom fiddled more with her napkin, "at first I was concerned. Actually," she said, "maybe a little jealous."

"Of this kind woman?"

"Suppose so. Silly, huh?"

Doreen remembered Melanie asking about her parents' marriage. Was it secure? Or was it Candy or Nat who'd asked? She couldn't remember. But now she was concerned.

She reached across the mini booth for two and clasped Mom's hands. They were clammy and cold, so she squeezed harder. "What is going on, Mom? You and Dad have been married for over fifty years."

"Not sure. Feel old and frumpy."

"You are not frumpy! And," Doreen summoned up all her faith, "you, besides me as the bride, is the most important woman in the wedding."

"Really? Why so?"

"First of all, you are the MOB." Doreen explained the acronym to her. "It's the role played by the woman who produced the bride, who gave her everything."

"I don't think I gave you much, but I tried, always tried."

"You gave me all, Mom, all. Especially my faith."

The omelets were served and they both dug in. Doreen had one more hurdle to cross with her mom.

"Please stay. Please let Connie design a beautiful gown for you."

"Okay. Maybe. Oh, okay. I guess I can take a few more days. Dad will be fine with Mrs. Murphy."

Doreen sighed with relief. But Mom chatted on.

"So, what is this I hear about a special promotion for a free wedding gown? If there's anything I can do to help I want to," she said. Seeing the confusion on Doreen's face she grinned. "Vivian told me."

Twenty-six

"Did you find out anything?" Vivian touched her hand on Bill's arm.

"Not yet. Too soon." He gently removed her hand. "Had to be a bit, uh a little, actually more than a little, deceptive."

"Oh."

"Not something I like to do. Not my style, or my morals."

"I know. But, maybe," she hesitated, "it was necessary? This time."

It was definitely a question Bill wanted to avoid, so he plunked his bulk on a counter chair. He rubbed his forehead with his palms, then slammed them on the marble. "I don't know what to do, Viv. For once I really don't know what to do, what is right."

"You want to save your son." Vivian rested her fingertips on his hand. She knew what was coming. She was prepared.

~

"Jaeda," Bill pleaded, "I need your advice."

The banker, the one who had been in the confidence of the Memory Men group that provided anonymous start-up sums to forthcoming entrepreneurs, the only one trusted with the group's secret, the one who had anonymously gifted Connie for her Winning Designs Boutique, replied with reluctance. "That's not my area, Bill."

"But, please, can you find out anything, anything at all?"

"I will try. As long as legally possible." Jaeda hung up the phone and rubbed his brow. He loved Big Bill, as everyone dubbed him, but this was out of his bailiwick, his sphere of operations, not his modus operandi. He didn't do sleuthing.

~

Connie cuddled little twin Larry and stroked doggie Jake with her free hand. "I don't know how or what to advise you, Jaed."

"I can't go against company policy. I won't. But," he kneaded his hands together, "there must be something I can do. Both Bills need to find out about this Marina woman making the paternal claim against Bill, Jr. Doreen needs to find out, too."

Connie jumped up, almost dropping little Larry. She laughed laying him down on the sofa. "Sorry, little guy. Just got an inspiration." Jake raised his head for an almost silent woof, then snuggled under the throw blanket in normal Min-Pin style.

"Do you remember we installed a camera after that woman tried to steal a gown?"

"Yeh. So?"

"Maybe there will be a photo on it of the Marina woman."

Jaeda didn't look too encouraged, but he said, "Okay. Try. Do you know how to bring it up?"

Connie fiddled on her computer. Nothing. "There is a way. Do we still have the instructions? The pamphlet that came with it?"

Jaeda rooted through the all-purpose kitchen junk drawer laughing.

"What's so funny?"

"The fact that we've never used it. Wasn't the idea of the camera to check it daily? Or at least weekly? To spy on our clients, even employees?"

"Employees!" Connie shouted. "Surely you trust Doreen," she said glaring at him.

"Don't be so upset, Con. Of course, given. But there might be a time in the future when we need to hire her an assistant, so even with thorough background checks . . ." His voice trailed off. "Here it is." He waved a booklet fanning her face.

"Good, Mr. Trustworthy, you look up the instructions!" She stomped away when she heard a twin whimper. Within minutes she returned. "Your son has a poopy diaper." She held her nose and stuck her tongue out at her husband, a half-grin on her face. "Your turn!"

~

"Dor, we found something. Something that might help."

Doreen held the phone away. Why was Connie shouting?

"Sorry for shouting, Dor. Excited."

"I think we found a picture of the Marina

woman on the store's security camera," Jaeda said, more calmly than Connie had.

"So?" Silence. "Don't mean to sound ungrateful, but I saw her with my own eyes. And," she said, "if you remember I have an almost photographic memory. How can the photo help?"

"Just look at this, please." Connie brought up the photo on her computer and forwarded it to Doreen. "Maybe something will grab you. Look carefully. Study everything about her."

Five minutes later Doreen sighed. "It's so vague. What am I looking for?"

"Everything. Look closely at her face, her shoes, her handbag, even her hair." Connie was getting impatient. She knew something was there that was puzzling, and she was pretty sure what.

Doreen scanned over the photo again, and suddenly gasped. "She's wearing a wig!"

"That's what I thought, too, but I wasn't sure." She concentrated on the photo again. "Yes, you can almost see the gray-blonde hairs at her forehead. Not a thirty-something woman with dark hair. Not the Marina that Bill described."

"Can you see any of her fingers, or part of one of her hands?"

"Yes. They look old and wrinkled. Not the hand of a thirty-year-old. Unless . . . someone was impersonating her. But," Doreen took a cleansing breath, "who would do that? For what?"

"Dor," Jaeda interrupted, "we need to send this photo to Big Bill for his inspection. He will know what to do. You okay with that?" After Doreen agreed, Jaeda clicked off the computer. He knew

Bill, Sr. had resources. Hopefully, he would use them.

Bill knew just about everyone. At least that is how the legend goes. He hoped he still did. Old friends are valuable.

Twenty-seven

How much value would Denny put on a forty-year friendship? Was he still working in IT, or retired? Did he still have connections? Bill said a prayer and dialed. Vivian touched his arm.

Bill didn't have much, but Denny provided him with some tidbits. He dialed Doreen on her landline. Denny was on his landline, too.

Jaeda and Connie picked up their landline phones in tandem. Doreen picked up hers being so glad she still had that option so they could all converse together.

"Got something." Big Bill's voice boomed across the landlines. "Hope it helps."

His friend had done extensive research on the Capelli family and discovered a tenuous connection to the famous shoe king, Manolo Blahnik.

Denny turned out to be a loyal friend thanking Bill for his support many years ago.

"But you were innocent."

"Not according to everyone, Bill. You were the

one who believed in me, who went to bat for me." His voice wobbled. "Now, let's get to the chase. Tell me all so I can help."

Bill explained the Marina situation explaining Bill, Jr. was the wrongly accused father of an illegitimate child. And how she was trying to compromise him and stop his wedding and ask for retribution.

"Sounds like blackmail," Denny said. "How long ago was this?" He paused before asking the next question. "Is this here in the United States?"

Bill forgot his nod couldn't be seen from California to Missouri. "Yep," he finally answered. "Just came up a few weeks before Bill and Doreen's wedding. Which," he added "they postponed. But the woman accusing Bill is Italian, belongs to a prominent family in Italy."

"We will fix this, have to," Denny said. Bill heard some clicking, computer sounds? When Denny finally spoke his voice was shaky again. "I remember little Bill. Nice kid, good morals, you raised him right, you and Mara. So sorry about her death." Another silence. "I know you have moved on. Happy for you."

"Thanks, Denny. Mara was the most important part of my life. She was my love who gave me Bill. But I am very happy now with a wonderful woman." This time he turned to touch Vivian's arm. She smiled with misty eyes.

~

"So," Jaeda said, "the woman who came in first was not Marina?"

"Probably not," Bill said. "She was not a young

woman. At least if the video part that shows her hand is telling the truth. Denny copied the hand and put it up anonymously on the internet. All responses said it was the hand of a seventy to eighty-year-old person. Not necessarily a woman, but we know it is. Maybe an aunt? At least someone in the family.

"Right, Denny?"

"Yes, everyone. Unless it's a young woman with a debilitating disease, it's a much older woman."

"I should have picked up on that," Doreen said. "Not as perceptive as I used to be. Am *I* getting old?"

They all needed that laugh. Connie hiccupped, Jaeda just laughed, and Bill guffawed. Denny snickered.

"Thanks for that, Dor," Connie said between hics.

"Glad to give you all some humor."

"Hey," Connie suddenly said. "I just remembered we didn't bring up the second woman, the woman Doreen thought might be the mother who is accusing Bill. She came in after the first woman while Natalie was minding the shop. Let's bring her photo up now." She did some keyboard clicking and suddenly a blurry image filled the screen.

"She ran out so quickly," Doreen said. "Almost faster than the first woman."

"Yes, but do you notice anything similar? Look closely."

"Maybe we should have Nat look at this." Doreen sounded confused. She called Nat.

"Coming right over. Gym is closed for the day. I am on it." Nat always sounded so positive.

~

Connie was getting impatient. The tautness in her blouse told her it was time to nurse the twins, a feat she had accomplished holding one each in the crooks of her arms. To distract herself she held the phone farther from her ear.

"Doreen, what is that sound?"

"What sound? Connection seems clear to me."

"That crackling sound. Like crunching."

"Oh, my dinner. Nachos, Cindy style, but not as good. Didn't have feta cheese."

"Nachos are your dinner?"

"Sometimes."

"What is breakfast?"

"Sometimes yogurt, sometimes nothing. Not hungry in morning."

"I am making a decision, Dor. Are you listening?"

"Uh, yeh."

"If you still want to be my employee, most importantly a model, you need to eat nourishing food, not chips. Got that?" Connie's voice was bordering on anger and she didn't wait for a response.

"So, Dor, here's the deal. You are beautiful, tall and slender, but lately you've been getting too skinny. So," Connie paused for a long breath, "you will start eating responsibly. BLD – breakfast, lunch, and dinner. Also snacks. You got that? Only *healthy* snacks from now on in the store.

"And," she paused again, "you will eat them. I

will be monitoring by email, phone, and now the in-store camera. Or, you will no longer be in my employ!"

"Why Con?"

"Because I hate skinny models!"

~

Natalie burst in the door and grabbed the phone from Doreen.

"Hey, Nat!"

"I want to hear all this, too."

"Well, you missed the best part about Connie threatening to fire me," Doreen grimaced.

"Shut UP! You can't be serious."

"I am, Nat, if she doesn't shape up and keep her shape." Connie's voice sang through the phone lines.

"I will see she does, Con. But stress sometimes takes its toll."

"Maybe we should Facetime," Connie said.

"NO. I don't want you to see me with Nacho cheese all over my face."

"Okay, trusting here. So, let's go over what Bill's friend Denny found."

Nat was remorseful she hadn't picked up on more about the woman. "I guess I was nervous taking over for Doreen. But that's no excuse. At least," she said, "Denny discovered something and Connie did, too, with the photo thing. Do you think any of this will help?"

Twenty-eight

Natalie gave Doreen a hug and breezed out. "So sorry for my blind spot about that woman."

"No big deal. Don't beat yourself up. I didn't pick up on the wig either."

Doreen clicked off the computer and kept munching, sharing bits of Fritos with Happy Arthur who scoffed them up. Probably the saltiness. Maybe not so good for dogs. She crumpled the bag and put it in the pantry. She would have more when she was reading before going to bed. Maybe Happy would be curled up asleep then. Mom, too. She heard faint snoring coming from the guest room. *Selfish me. I didn't even say goodnight.* But neither had Mom.

Did anyone really understand what she was going through with Bill and the horrible woman accusing him? Her heart sang when she heard the bing of a message from him, until she opened it.

A breakup text message? No. Must be wrong. Bill wouldn't do something so cowardly. But like the time he cursed, he just did.

She pushed the erase button, grabbed Happy, and slunk to bed to cuddle. Thank goodness she had adopted a dog!

~

"He did what?" Natalie was incensed the next morning, almost shouting.

"Said it was time to let go, find other options. What do you think he meant?"

Nat could hear Doreen sniffling. Not a good sign. She grouped for words and finally said, "He's scared, confused."

"So am I, Nat."

"But, he's a guy. And guys always want to fix things."

"He's not fixing this . . . this travesty. Maybe he's right. Maybe it is time to part ways."

"No, Dor, you need to answer him," Natalie was adamant. "You need to, must, and tell him what his dad's friend found out. Maybe that will jog a memory, or at least give him some perspective."

~

Doreen's hand shook as it hovered over her phone. Should she message Bill? Why, when he had basically broken up with her? She had nothing to apologize for.

Her text was simple, pleading ignorance. As if she hadn't understood what he meant. She sat back and waited. Too long. He wasn't answering. His loss. Time to take Happy Arthur for a walk to clear her brain. Fresh air always helped, didn't it? She took her phone with her. She hated to see people walking and chatting on the phone instead of breathing in the sea air. But this was an emergency, wasn't it?

"I can't do this, Nat. It's been two hours and he hasn't texted me back."

When Doreen and Happy got back from their walk Nat pulled out all the stops and connected them to all the Candy Canes via the shared phone line. The first to pick up was Cindy in Costa Rica.

"What is going on? I feel so out of the loop." Cindy's voice trembled. "I can't process this. Bill breaking up with you over a sham?"

"Perfect word, Cindy. I'm sure that's what it is." Nat went over what Big Bill's friend had learned about the Capelli family's connection to Manolo Blahnik. "Not cast in stone, but a pretty sure bet."

"I agree," Noelle said. "This can't be real. This Miranda woman has to be a gold digger."

"I agree, too. This is a set up for money. Almost blackmail," Candy said chiming in.

"Somehow," Melanie said, "we need to flush her out, expose her. Any ideas?"

Twenty-nine

Big Bill and his friend Denny had a plan. Would it work?

Connie advertised and Doreen set it up. Next week Winning Designs would have a special promotion for a free designer wedding gown. Because of the Capelli family's suspected connection to Manolo Blahnik, and Doreen noticing one of the mysterious women who came into the boutique was wearing the famous designer's shoes, the Candy Cane group with Denny's help put two and two together. Would it work and bring the mysterious women back?

Connie, as owner of the shop, decided on the particulars of the deceptive promotion based on what Jaeda called "a far-flung ploy." Would it reach the right person, tempt the woman trying to deceive Doreen and Bill? None of them were sure, but as Connie said, "Do nothing, get nothing."

Anyone who wore Manolo Blahnik shoes into the shop would receive a free custom designed wedding gown. The shop wouldn't sell them because it doesn't sell shoes, but it was a statement of distinction, of affluence, and of ego. They all prayed it would work.

The gown would come with a tiara. Doreen sniffed at that. She hated crowns. Floating, billowing veils were lovely, but tiaras were for pretend royalty. She would never wear one.

It was a huge risk because neither Connie nor Doreen knew if any of their established divas owned a pair of the designer's exclusive shoes. Hopefully, no one in the Newport Beach area did. Winning Designs clients tended more toward French and American shoes. Shoes seldom showed under long gowns. Although money was seldom an object, it was put into extravagant attire that others could see. And the latest trend was to wear sneakers hidden by the gowns so the bride wouldn't trip and could dance her heart out at the reception. Doreen had always laughed at the idea, but now with her own wedding on the horizon, it made sense. Maybe she could dance. Maybe she could find her groove. If she wore sneakers.

The announcement went out everywhere, on Facebook and Twitter, the *Los Angeles Times* and many local city newspapers, also TV. Seven women, actually more with Vivian and Marion now on board, prayed it would work. Would it?

Melanie turned on CNN. Wow! The female news anchor said, "Fun announcement. A boutique, Winning Designs in Corona del Mar, Newport Beach is having a special. If you want a free custom wedding gown and appear in a pair of famous

Italian designer Manolo Blahnik shoes, you are in!" The brief announcement led into a commercial for cereal.

Thirty

"What's happening?" Big Bill's voice boomed loudly into Connie's ear. She held the phone away.

"Bill," she said calmly, or at least tried to, "It doesn't start until tomorrow. Wednesday."

"Does Billy know about this?"

"He should. It went out on Facebook, email lists, and Instagram. I think he has all of those."

~

Bill, Jr. rubbed his eyes and pinched his nose. The TV announcement stuck in his brain. What was going on? Where did the shoe thing come from? Ridiculous. Who wore those shoes? Then it hit him. Was Dad behind this?

He collapsed on his bed and a few curses snuck out. Fortunately, no one could hear them. Except Him. Well, God. Smacking his forehead and running fingers through his hair he finally got it.

"I got it! Now what Lord? Am I supposed to respond? Should I be there when this takes place? If it takes place?"

~

Natalie let herself in the back door with the code. She had agreed to help Doreen for a few more days. Bryce was back and taking over the fitness schedule in the gym and Momma Claire, as she called her, was helping with everything else. Vivian even offered to come in to help check members in, set up equipment, and wipe down. Natalie wasn't too comfortable with that. After all Vivian was almost seventy. But the thing she felt most uncomfortable with was the Big Bill thing. She called Doreen.

"I know you are worried about him. He can be intrusive, but that's because he cares. Let him in when he comes, but secure him in the back. Among the wrappings and delivery boxes and all the discarded stuff." She laughed. "Remember this was his idea."

Natalie adjusted her skirt and looked down at her Nikes. Not expected attire for a high-end boutique, but comfy and what she wore daily to her gym. At exactly ten, the bell buzzed. She panicked for a minute. Doreen wasn't here yet. Should she press the buzzer to open the door?

Doreen slid in through the back entrance and placed a hand on Nat's shoulder.

"Whew. Thank goodness. I wasn't sure what to do."

Doreen smiled, pushed the buzzer, and the front door opened.

~

"Good morning, Madam. Welcome to Winning Designs. How may I help you?" Doreen extended a slender hand.

The other woman smiled, slightly. "I am here," she said in a heavy accent, "for zee free weedding gown."

Doreen looked at her shoes and made a decision.

"Ma'am, may I see one of your shoes please? Before I give away an exclusive wedding gown, I need to be sure you are wearing Manolo Blahnik shoes. I'm sure you understand."

Instead of the woman removing a shoe she spun on one of them and raced to the door to be buzzed out. "So much for victim number one." Doreen slumped into a chair and grinned at Natalie. "Maybe next time. Or the next. Or, maybe not ever."

"What's happening?" Big Bill's voice boomed from the back room. "I am tired of sitting on this folding chair. Tell me what's going on."

Doreen went back and gathered his big hands in hers. "Nothing yet, Bill. Just one customer, a hopeful wannabe."

"How long do I have to sit here in this miserable chair? I am not used to waiting."

Thirty-one

"Maybe the promos didn't work, reach the right people. Or person," he added. "Maybe this was all a mistake, a fly in the ointment." Big Bill squirmed in the folding chair. It didn't accommodate his bulk, nor his personality. Vivian, he thought, would tell him to calm down and rest in the Lord. He called her. "Need support, Viv."

She prayed Psalm 62:5, "Yes my soul, find rest in God; my hope comes from him," then she whispered, "Buff up, Bill. This was your idea. Own it."

The buzzer sounded again. Doreen looked at the camera. The woman seemed innocent enough so she buzzed her in. She seemed to be in her forties, attractive with dark hair swept up. Doreen focused on her shoes. They looked like the right ones, but no telling without examining one. She did the standard offering her hand and greeting. Then her hand got cold.

"I am here to apologize." The attractive woman

lowered her head while clasping Doreen's hand. "My family is wrong."

Doreen cocked her head. What was this woman saying?

"You not understand?"

"No. Sorry."

"My niece is money hungry. She is also a liar. You understand now?"

"No, but I am willing to listen, if what you are saying is the truth."

"I tell you zee trut . . . truth. Sorry my English ees bad."

"That's all right, but please go on, Ms.?"

For a moment the question hung in the air. Finally, the woman spoke in a low whisper. Doreen held her breath.

"My name ees Sofia. I represent the Capelli family. Yes, I am wearing a pair of Manolo Blahnik shoes." She took off one and offered it to Doreen with both hands like a gift. "'But," she continued, "I am here to make amends."

Doreen turned the shoe over in her hands. She hoped they were Manolo Blahnik shoes. They were definitely his special signature shoes, but his signature label was on the inside. She had read extensively about the designer's shoes since doing this promotion. Especially the famous and singular Carolyne. The shoe handed to her was leather and the label was on the instep in blue and black. An earlier version of the Carolyne? Perhaps. She remembered reading the "Manolo' is blue and 'Blahnik' is in black. Some people will see that and think the shoe is counterfeit," the website said, "but it's just a sign the shoe is older." She had also read the two-toned label only appeared on the Carolyne style. Who is or was Carolyne?

"How did you get these? How do I know they are genuine?"

The woman tried to suppress a laugh by holding her hand over her mouth. "I am zee direct descendent of Manolo Blahnik. He was my grandfather's brother. Yes, they are genuine. They are real. Look at zee label. I can explain eef necessary."

Doreen decided to trust Sofia, if that really was her name. This woman seemed much more genuine than the others. No fancy hairdo, simple nails with clear polish, a Jessica Simpson purse. No phoniness, no pretensions. The woman smiled again and opened her arms.

Doreen hesitated for a moment, then threw her arms around Sophia. But she couldn't resist asking, "How do you plan to make amends?"

She handed the shoe back to Sophia. Why did that footwear feel like fire in her hands?

"May we sit?" Sophia asked.

"Of course. Sorry I didn't suggest it." Doreen pulled out two chairs and sat near the other woman. She extended her hand again clasping Sophia's in hers.

"Let me begin weeth a long story," Sophia said. Doreen nodded, anxious to hear it.

~

"My pawpaw, my grandfather," Sophia lowered her head and blushed. "He was special to me. But even though he was the original designer, he couldn't claim it."

Doreen squeezed the other woman's hand

lightly. "Go on."

Sophia nodded. "He and his brother, how you say it, Bro?" she giggled nervously. "They have disagreement. Fight."

"What did they fight about?" Doreen couldn't contain her curiosity.

"A woman," Sophia said simply. "Always a woman."

Thirty-two

Doreen rooted around in her nightstand. "Finally! Success!" She clutched the coolness and squeezed it in her hand. Slapping the herb infused pillow on her eyes, she sighed. She desperately wanted to sleep, but the conversation with Sophia took over.

"What woman?"

"I really can't say, because I don't know. Eees history, but," she said, "history has a way of repeeating."

The woman, Sophia, really hadn't told her anything. Just rumors and legends. Family legends. The only comment she made that peeked Doreen's interest was, "She is a liar." Who? Was she referring to Miranda? It all happened so fast, none of it was clear. Did Big Bill hear it, too?

He had burst out of the back room just as the shop door clicked shut. "What the heck is going on? Who was that woman? What did she say?"

Doreen and Natalie stumbled over words at the same time. But he wasn't appeased. After all, Bill had set this scheme up, and he was getting no results.

Doreen turned over in bed and snuggled her cheek into the pillow. Remembering she had read doing so was bad for the skin, she sighed and shifted onto her back. Suddenly, she felt a flop between her legs. Arthur stretched his legs to fit between hers. He snorted and snuggled in. So much for sleeping alone. At least he didn't snore, yet.

~

Bill picked up on the first ring. Denny.

"Another idea. I think I can find a way to expose her." Bill could almost see the grin on Denny's face.

"Gotta tell Doreen so she's prepared," Bill said.

"Agreed. But, let's wait a bit until I'm sure how to do this."

They were playing How to Catch a Thief in cyberspace. Would it work? Bill hoped so.

"I got her on social media. Don't know why I didn't think about that before," Denny said. "I don't do much of it, so I had to join Facebook so I could go on hers. This is what I found."

Bill looked at the text and photos Denny had copied and sent to him in email. He didn't do social media either, so he was confused. "What does all this mean? How can we use it against her?"

"Tell Connie and Doreen to check it out. I'm sure they are on Facebook and Twitter and Instagram. They will figure it out." Denny clicked off. Bill was alone with his confusing thoughts.

~

"I never thought to do that," Connie said. "I

hardly ever check my personal Facebook page, just the Winning Designs account, and then only occasionally." She did the Connie sigh. "I suppose I should check it out more often, even daily, to see what people are saying about my designs and the boutique."

"Me, too." Doreen booted up her laptop, signed in to her seldom used Facebook account, looked at her timeline and squealed. "I can't believe I didn't think to look. She's threatening me, accusing me, accusing Bill. What can we do?" Her voice was filled with anger.

"What does 23 and Me mean? What is that?"

Bill called Denny again. He was the man with the tech answers.

When Denny picked up he laughed. "I guess no one in your family is much of a Facebook user."

Bill snorted. "Why should we? For me I don't need to contact or connect with random people. I have all I want right here."

"I understand and respect that, but it is the twenty-first century, Buddy."

"Just tell us what to look for, what to do. By the way, Doreen and Connie are on the phone, too."

"Oh, one of those shared landlines?" Denny asked.

"Okay. Go to this link and carefully read through it. Then tell me what you see."

~

Bill, Sr. didn't understand. Why is there a child in a wheelchair? He figured out to look for the date and time it was posted. A year ago? What! "Denny, help please. I am confused."

"I will try. If the photo of the child was a year ago, and if it was supposed to be current, the child was only a toddler then," Denny said with conviction. "Bill, Jr. hasn't been in Italy for years. Right?"

"Not for at least ten."

"So, the woman – Miranda – is trying to scam you."

"But how do we know the photo of the child isn't eons old? Or if it's the child in question?"

"We don't. But why would she put a picture of a toddler on her Facebook page just a few days ago? Doesn't make sense unless it's not 'the' child and she has another one."

"What is the child's disability? Does she say?"

"Really, Bill, you need to get better at this. Let me go back and see."

Bill took a hard gulp and swallowed Denny's comment. After all his old friend was helping him.

"Okay." Denny came back on the phone. "The photo was posted twelve days ago about the time Miranda called Bill Junior. But," he emphasized, "there is no way to tell when it was actually taken. So, back to square one.

"Oh, to answer your question, it's a genetic disease. Marfan Syndrome is passed down through the father." Denny whooshed a sigh. "Does young Bill or you have that in your family history, or your genes?"

"How would I know? Never heard of it until now," he bellowed. "I am more than frustrated and confused."

"Look it up, Bill. Learn about it. Be sure."

Denny hung up, probably frustrated, too.

Bill pulled Vivian to his side. She was much better at this Googling thing than he.

"Bill, we need to call in the troops. They are younger, understand this better than we do."

"I agree," Connie said still on the group call. "How about you, Doreen?"

"I think we need to call the others. Maybe some of them use Facebook more than us."

Thirty-three

"Look closely at the eyes in the child in the wheelchair," Connie said. "Yes, I read up on it. Rare disease, weird. I just finished reading everything about it. Bill," she said with conviction, "I can't see how Bill Junior could have had any role in this. Even if he did have sex with the Marina woman. This is the latest I read. '. . . if a child born to two blue-eyed parents does not have blue eyes, then the blue-eyed father is not the biological father.' This child in the photo has brown eyes. This is preposterous."

Bill, Sr. wiped his brow. It was time for a confrontation. Should he try to get through to the Marina woman, or just let it go? He trusted his son and was sure Doreen trusted him, too. What a quandary. He thought about that old phrase between a rock and a hard place. That's where he was now.

He heard gentle woofing in the background. Melanie? Her dog? Maybe he needed gentle right now. He asked, grateful she was still on the line.

"Right here, Bill. Yes, you heard Lola. I also heard what Connie said. I agree. Time to bite the bullet and let it go."

"You think I, we, should just ignore it? Pretend it didn't happen."

He respected Melanie since she had been so graciously forgiven by Doreen after the devastating accident that took inches off of Doreen's leg. Doreen was the hero. His future daughter-in-law, one he loved very much.

"I think it's worth a try, Bill. This woman has gone too far. If she goes farther, I would get legal advice and insist on a DNA test."

Vivian touched his elbow. "I agree, darling. This is crazy. Almost as if the woman is clutching at straws. I understand," she sighed, "a mother will do almost anything to help her child. But this has gone too far. It's ruining two other wonderful people's futures."

Connie chimed in again. "Bill, this woman sounds desperate, but not genuine, not really sincere. She is making a frantic attempt to salvage a bad situation. She has no basis in logic or fact. Just a hope. Sadly, a false one. But have you thought about all the resources she has? The money behind the Manolo Blahnik shoes? Certainly she would have access to that. Sorry, gotta go. Diaper change time."

Bill was not comfortable just letting it go. He had to know more. Where was his son in all this?

~

"Uh, hi, Dad."

"Where the rudgyfudgy have you been? The

girls and I have been dealing with this Miranda situation, but not a word from you. After all, Bill, it's your future to consider."

Vivian again touched Bill's arm. "Stop huffing, dear. Bad for your blood pressure."

"My BP's fine. 104 over 60. But my faith in my son isn't," he whispered.

"Don't know, Dad. Maybe she drugged me?"

"That's possible, dear. He was only a boy," Vivian said.

"If that's so, if even possible, it's against the law. And you have no involvement," Bill said with conviction. "Do you? Did you?"

Thirty-four

It was time to let it go. Everyone agreed. But before he did, Bill checked the woman's Facebook page again and was totally flummoxed. The picture of the boy was gone. He called Denny.

"Yep, gone, Bill. She took it down. Could mean one of several things," he continued. "Maybe she got negative comments, maybe her family told her to ditch it, maybe she got scared or found religion."

Bill snuffed at that.

Denny said, "Don't get huffy. I meant maybe guilt took over."

"I hope so, since she is the guilty one."

"You want to pursue this more? Or let it go?"

"Don't know. Need advice." He clicked off the phone and settled in his recliner to pray Jeremiah 29:11. The answer came.

Epilogue
Six months later

The two Bills, father and son, as well as all the Candy Canes and Denny frequently checked the Miranda Corelli's Facebook page. Even Marion Zimmer had learned how to do it. After several months, they stopped.

"I give up!" Connie, Doreen and Melanie almost said in tandem during a group phone call. Natalie, Noelle and Candy laughed.

Cindy protested, "I still feel out of the loop so far away."

"Blessed you are!" Candy said. "Just focus on little Robby and keep up those Bible studies you do for the locals. We still want to hear about a church planting in Costa Rica."

~

Typical soft pre-wedding music was playing while guests were being seated. Marion Zimmer wiggled a bit in her MOB gown. Connie had designed it to camouflage her hips and tummy and emphasize her neck. Why had she been reluctant? This was the loveliest dress she'd ever worn.

She beamed at Vivian radiant in a swirling lavender frock. Vivian touched her slightly graying upswept hair and grinned. Marion grinned back, two loving mothers. For a moment, before their husbands joined them, they clasped hands. Hugs would come later.

~

The long-awaited wedding went off without a hitch. Natalie was hugging and holding Happy Arthur. He deserved to be part of the fun since he had gifted Doreen with the tennis shoe that might save her dancing dilemma. Nat wasn't sure who hoped more, her or the little dog.

The bride glided down the aisle on her father's arm in a billowing lily-white gown accented with lavender lace, an exclusive Connie design that would never be replicated. Cindy couldn't be there, but Melanie, Candy, Connie, Noelle, and Natalie looked ethereal in the palest of lavender. The alternate mother figure Clair took charge of the arrangements with the wedding coordinator at the Newport Beach Fashion Island Hotel. Doreen had given Billy full command with Claire and Vivian's guidance and help. Such a relief. After all the wedding chatter, plans, and arguments she'd listened to for years from clients, she was not excited about planning. Just eager to be in Billy's arms forever.

She was still worried about the wedding dance. How could she dance with her love in a prosthetic shoe, and with her father who had flown in three days ago, just in time for the rehearsal dinner and hugs? Mom had seemed a little miffed, but Doreen learned she'd picked him up at John Wayne Airport, pecked him on the cheek, and drove him to Doreen's condo in the rental car she had learned to drive.

"Wow, Mom, you are becoming a twenty-first century woman!"

"Gotta do what I can do. Keep up with the times," she laughed hugging Doreen. "Are you ready? How are you doing about the dancing part? Have you found your groove yet?"

Doreen shrugged. "I will get through it. I know Dad will just shuffle, but Billy is a fabulous dancer. We should have taken an Arthur Murray course."

"Why didn't you?"

"Time. Scared maybe. Embarrassed."

"You will whirl beautifully," Marion said. "I have it from a Higher Authority." She touched the silver cross at her throat, kissed Doreen, and left her standing to wonder.

The special music was playing as she and Bill entered the reception, the music that introduced them as a couple. He led her with his strong hand and pulled out her chair. His smile glowed and his azure eyes shined with love. She gathered the luxurious skirt of the gown around her trembling legs. She knew the first thing on the agenda was the wedding couple dance.

Stumbling was not an option. She kicked off the silver shoes, the ones she had worn in so many friends' weddings, and tugged on her workout shoes hidden under the tablecloth. Not very classy, but the best option she had. The laces on the left one were still damp and tangled from when Happy chewed on them. She laughed at the memory. His little face looked so sincere like he was trying to give her a hint. She got it. She would dance better in these shoes.

Since she had gladly given Billy the right to all the details of the wedding, from guest invitations (which she suspected Vivian handled), to timing, and dance, and dinner choices (salmon, yea!), she was free. Except for the dance part. Could she fake it?

The band leader announced the first dance, the dance for the bride and groom. She had asked for her favorite song, from her favorite movie. "'I've Had the Time of My Life. . . Don't put Baby in a corner.'"

She loved that song because she felt as if she had been left in a corner, especially since her accident, and long before in high school when she had been a wallflower. Memories flooded her. Her high school prom that she finally went to with a few friends, not even good friends, but girls who had agreed to include her since she offered to drive. Then left her standing alone.

Finally, a boy with enormous glasses and a leg brace approached her. She had been uncertain, but it seemed unkind to refuse him. A few students laughed, but the boy grinned and held her closer. They twirled and their feet refused to stop. He led her back to the chairs pushed against the wall of the gym. He bowed and left with a fleeting kiss on the back of her hand.

Suddenly she was a princess. Just for a moment, thanks to that boy in glasses and brace. Had he been an angel? One that shared her future? All she remembered was he was very tall and very blonde and very handsome with cheeks sculpted at angles under his ears. At the time she thought he could be a model, even with the glasses and brace. She never knew his name.

Billy took her hand again. His smile said it would be okay.

The band started playing the song slowly and softly as if waiting for something else to happen. How unusual. She lifted her veil higher above the sparkling diamond-studded tiara Billy had asked for.

"All brides wear one," he'd said.

A small compensation for the man she loved.

She was tying the laces on her brown shoes when she heard a whimper. Happy Arthur stood at her heels quivering. His little face tilted and his eyes held a question. Did dogs do that?

She looked back to Natalie who had promised to hold him. Nat shrugged and spread her arms. Arthur scampered back to Nat. Was his job done?

She started to rise from the Sweetheart Table and felt a touch on her arm.

A woman with long flowing dark hair placed something in her hands. A pair of Manolo Blahnik shoes in glittering silver.

"They will make you dance," she said. "There is even a lift in the left one." But before she disappeared in the crowd she looked back and whispered, "I am so sorry."

Doreen kicked off her ugly shoes and slipped on the beautiful silver shoes. She waved back to the woman, rose to take Billy's hand, and twirled. She had finally found her groove.

THE END

About Bonnie Engstrom

Bonnie and her husband Dave of 54 years reside in Arizona near four of their six grandchildren. The other two live in Costa Rica on the beach. Pura Vida! See the whole crew at www.bonnieengstrom.com.
Bonnie and Dave raised their three children in Newport Beach, California with five cats, Luciano Pavarotti the masked love bird and Jake the Min-Pin whose picture is on the cover of *Connie's Silver Shoes*. Their rescued dog Lola is on the cover of *Melanie's Blue Skirt*. All of their animals were rescued because they believe "You can't buy love, but you can rescue it."

Happy Arthur, the rescued dog on the cover of *Doreen Finds Her Groove* belongs to a dear friend, Lisa.

Books by Bonnie Engstrom

Butterfly Dreams

BONNIE ENGSTROM

A Winning Recipe

A Cup of Love

Her Culinary Catch

The Matchmaking Wedding Planner

Restoring Love at Christmastime

The Candy Cane Girls Series:

Noelle's Christmas Wedding

Cindy's Perfect Dance

Candy's Wild Ride

Connie's Silver Shoes

Natalie's Deception

Melanie's Blue Skirt

Melanie's Ghosts

www.ingramcontent.com/pod-product-compliance
Lightning Source LLC
LaVergne TN
LVHW010328070526
838199LV00065B/5691

The phone call to Doreen's fiancé Bill is frightening. The woman swears he has a child. Bill vows he never had a romantic relationship with the Italian shoe heiress. Is he lying? Could the woman have seduced him during his modeling stint for the famous motorcycle company? Maybe Doreen should put off their wedding plans until the truth comes out.

Doreen's friendship group, the Candy Canes, gather around her to pray. She's a nervous wreck until she adopts Happy Arthur. Will the little fluffy canine help her take her mind off her troubles?

Bill's dad does some sleuthing on social media and comes up with an elaborate idea to expose the Italian woman. Will it work?

Doreen's biggest fear about her forthcoming wedding is how will she do the first dance with her handsome groom on her shorter leg. Maybe she should follow the latest trend other brides are doing and wear tennis shoes for their first dance. Will her little dog Happy help when he presents her with one? Would the comfy shoes help her find her groove?

Bonnie and her husband Dave of 54 years reside in Arizona near four of their six grandchildren. The other two live in Costa Rica on the beach. Pura Vida! See the whole crew at www.bonnieengstrom.com.

Bonnie and Dave raised their three children in Newport Beach, California with five cats, Luciano Pavarotti the masked love bird and Jake the Min-Pin whose picture is on the cover of Connie's Silver Shoes. Their rescued dog Lola is on the cover of Melanie's Blue Skirt. All of their animals were rescued because they believe "You can't buy love, but you can rescue it."